MRS KHAN AND THE W.I. BUCKET LIST

Mrs Khan and the W.I. Bucket List

by
Polly J. Fry

Published in 2022 by
RHR, 8 Brancepeth Gardens, Buckhurst Hill, IG9 5JL

Interior Layout by designforwriters.com
Cover design, Raven Print and Design, Cowes, IW, PO31

Contact Polly J. Fry: pollyjfrywriter@gmail.com

AUTHOR'S NOTE

The Tales of Mrs Khan appeared in a book of short stories called *Wyddershyns*. Various people read about her antics and asked to know more, not just about what she was up to herself but also the other people who shared her adventures. Did the Bucket List continue once we left her behind in ShortStoryLand and did all the entries come to fruition? What happened to Val and Lawrence Ford, to say nothing of young Lally and her little daughter Chelsea?

The Prologue to this novel was the first story in the series and introduces not just Mrs Khan but shows where the inspiration for the Bucket List came from. She's not based on anyone in particular but snippets of memory have been utilised from time to time, and I'd like to thank all those lovely women who sparked her creation for crossing my path. She's pretty cosmopolitan and belongs to nowhere, really, with the exception of her beloved Stackton-on-Sea.

Mrs Khan started off being Pakistani but as everyone who read her tales in *Wyddershyns* assumed she was Indian, she migrated for the purposes of this novel, moving again towards the end. She became a sort South Asian Everywoman, who in her understated and modest way, saves the day on many occasions. I hope that it's clear that Mrs Khan has been both conceived – by me – and received with great affection by those who have read about her adventures; and as you'll see, she's the inspiration for many more.

I don't belong to a WI, as I have no time to get involved but I very much hope that WIs up and down the land operate in the same way as the Stackton-on-Sea branch. Those women of my acquaintance who are members find it enriches their lives enormously and I trust that the support and camaraderie shared by the women presented here are as much a part of membership as – dare I venture – jam and Jerusalem, if these last are, indeed, still a part of W.I. life. I've never really seen why anyone would object – I make my own jam as much as possible and there's nothing like Parry's rousing score to get air flowing through the lungs and oxygen coursing through the veins, even if we're not in accord with the sentiments it presents; but I know not everyone would agree with me. I guess it depends on how literally you take Blake's words.

One last point: by the time I discovered many people were mispronouncing the name Ghaus, Mrs Khan's younger son had been part of my life for too long for me to rename him. As the name is Arabic in origin, I would be unable to reproduce the alphabet anyway and his name would never be accurately represented. I decided to spell it phonetically, so that it would be read accurately through-out. Hence, Gos. I hope this will not offend.

I hope you enjoy the daily exploits of Mrs Khan and her friends as much as I enjoyed creating them.

Polly J. Fry

PROLOGUE

CLOSE TO THE HEART

Mrs Khan had been dreaming of playing the harp since childhood but it had never happened; and as we know, everything starts with a dream. 'Time to take action,' she thought, and got down to the serious business of making plans.

First find your harp. 'How?' She wondered. As Mrs Khan had been picturing herself playing a wonderful concerto with a big orchestra, she thought she'd write to one of them to ask them what to do.

'Dear Bristol Symphonic Orchestra', she wrote. 'I want to play harp. Wanted to even when a child. Can you advise please?' She pressed 'send' and got on with the everyday business of sorting out the washing.

Mr Khan had been gone a long time now, so she couldn't talk to him about it direct. Instead, she spoke to him in her head. 'I know we always said it would take up too much space and time but I'm on my own now and time's getting on. I'm going to do what I have to do.'

The rest of the day was nothing special. She put the washing away, went to the shops for provisions – only once a week now she lived alone – and had a chat with her neighbour, Gloria, who was worried about her son. Gloria was *always* worried about her son and Mrs Khan was grateful again that her own sons had never given her anything to worry about.

She cooked her supper and settled down to watch television. It was an ordinary sort of evening for viewing: soap operas, people getting murdered in the most bizarre and elaborate ways with some clever chap (who Mrs Khan secretly thought was rather dishy and was the reason she watched it) solving it all by being very sensible and logical; and then a chat programme with lots of people she'd never heard of but gathered were frightfully famous and doing exciting things. The audience thought so, anyway, if the applause and laughter were anything to go by.

Before going to bed, she checked her emails, as she did every night. Gos often emailed her to give her updates on his life in America with photos of the grandchildren, now virtually grown up. She loved getting them and treasured every single one. Tonight, however, things were different.

'Dear Mrs Khan', it read, 'thank you for contacting us. We have forwarded your email to Lawrence Ford, one of our harpists. He will be in touch with you in due course. Good luck with your endeavour.' Mrs Khan's day had turned into something special after all.

***

Lawrence was a bit surprised to receive an email like this out of the blue. Surely, there were loads of music hubs and centres around now, but, he supposed, the harp's a bit of a specialist niche and even the best music schools didn't necessarily have access to a harpist. When you put it into the context of the *real* world, the harp world is quite small.

He'd had these enquiries before and it always came to nothing. They'd buy themselves an expensive harp, in spite of him telling them they should start by hiring to see how they got on. Then, they'd have a few lessons and discover that it was a lot harder than they thought it would be and gave up in possession of an instrument they'd never be able to sell. Still, it was no skin off his nose. If she wanted to waste time and money, what was it to him? So, he too took to electronic communication to further Mrs Khan's dream:

'Dear Mrs Khan. Thank you for your enquiry. If you are serious in your quest to learn the harp, I am happy for you to come to my home for a lesson. I have a variety of harps and you are welcome to try them out to see what sort might be best for you. The price of a lesson is fifty pounds. Lawrence Ford.' He pressed 'send' and thought no more of it.

* * *

Mrs Khan couldn't believe her eyes. She was due for the W.I. meeting that afternoon and they were having a talk on '*The Life of a Barber Surgeon in the Eighteenth Century*'. Not really her caldron of octopus but she liked the company and the tea and cake always meant she only needed a snack in the evening. She got herself ready more haphazardly than was her wont, because she was distracted. Maybe this was the start of something big.

Before setting out, she sent her response.

'Dear Mr Ford. I much appreciate your interest in my query. I would love to examine your harps and have lesson with you. Please advise possible times and how to get to your home. With best wishes to you and to your family. I hope you are all very well. Mrs Khan.'

* * *

They arranged a meeting for the following Tuesday. Mrs

Khan had already decided she'd splash out on a taxi. She really didn't want to be late for such an important occasion and it was never a good idea to rely on public transport if time was critical.

It took a veritable age to get there. Every single traffic light was against them, the queues of traffic were ridiculous and pedestrians kept stepping in to the road so the driver had to stop. If that wasn't enough, he wanted to talk all the time about the state of the nation, the state of the world and even the state of his bunions. At last they pulled up outside quite an imposing, double-fronted house with at least three storeys and a wrought iron gate – beautifully fashioned in the shaped of swan – leading onto the garden path, which in its turn led up to the door. He was a lot taller than he looked online, his hair a great deal greyer. Indeed, there was considerably less of it than the photograph suggested. Still, she wasn't going to hold it against him that he wanted to present a smart image to the computer-using public.

Lawrence's heart dropped when he saw Mrs Khan. 'This woman must be in her 70s,' he thought. 'What on earth does she think she's doing starting the harp at her age?' – at least as old as he was himself, but he'd been playing since he was a child. Poor Lawrence had a somewhat jaded outlook on life. Nobody knew why, unless it was to do with his wife running off with the orchestra manager some years back but these days, such events were commonplace and people generally got over them in time. 'Come in, dear lady,' he said. 'How lovely to meet you.'

Mrs Khan followed him to his music room and stepped into what she could only describe as Harp Wonderland. There were instruments of all sizes: large, small, some you could rest on your knees, some with levers, some with pedals, all beautifully decorated and clearly lovingly maintained. Momentarily, it took her breath away.

'We haven't talked yet about what you want to achieve with your harp playing,' he said. 'Have you any ideas?'

'Not at all,' said Mrs. Khan. 'I will take your advice and follow your instructions.'

'My advice,' thought Lawrence, 'would be to learn the ukulele.' But of course, he wasn't rude enough to say so.

After a brief discussion, he led Mrs Khan to a full-sized pedal harp more in the hope of putting her off than thinking there'd be any hope of her being able to master it. She sat down and he explained how to hold it and how to place her fingers. Immediately, she started playing arpeggios, scales and even short tunes. He watched open-mouthed as the strings came alive under her fingers.

'Where did you learn before?' Lawrence asked her.

'I have had no lessons, but have watched playing for many years, looked on the net for instruction and imagined this moment since childhood. This is my dream come true'.

He'd noticed how her eyes lit up as soon as the instrument touched her shoulder and the atmosphere that emanated from her person changed from anxious to calm and happy. After all, the harp vibrates close to the heart. Maybe he'd been wrong to judge. Being in her 70s wasn't going to be a barrier in any way at all. Or so he hoped.

**

The months went by. Mrs Khan never did call him Lawrence, in spite of him keep insisting; and he never discovered her first name. She steadfastly declined his offer of refreshments and although she regularly brought him the most wonderful cakes and biscuits – all homemade – she would never join him in an impromptu tea party or stay a minute longer than the hour they had arranged.

His colleagues started noticing that he was softer, somehow, and less prickly. No-one asked him why, of course, because it simply wouldn't do.

He loved teaching Mrs Khan. These sessions were refreshing, as she was so full of life and enthusiasm. She'd never be able to read music, but he only had to play something to her and she could reproduce it, key changes and all and with lovely nuances in the delivery; and they improvised together all the time. He'd offered to waive her lesson fee, because, as he pointed out, he wasn't really teaching her anything. They were just making music together, and beautiful music at that. She'd refused – he'd already lent her a harp with no charge and she couldn't take advantage of his good nature.

***

'Mr. Ford,' she started one afternoon. 'I can no longer impose on your kind disposition.' His heart dropped to his boots, thinking that she was going to stop coming to him for these brief meetings. 'You have been good enough to lend me a beautiful harp. I must either purchase this from you or you must tell me where I can go to acquire an equally pleasing instrument for myself.'

Relieved, he gave her a price for his harp that was a tiny fraction of what it was worth,

'Very good, Mr Ford. I will bring money with me next time we meet.' She went home that evening thrilled that she was going to be able to play it for ever, with no worries about Mr Ford needing to take it back. Lawrence, for his part, was equally relieved that his relationship with this lovely sensitive woman and very special musician was not going to be brought to an end.

**

At the first meeting of the W.I. after the summer break, the President bounced up to Mrs Khan and welcomed her in her usual animated fashion. 'Mrs Khan,' she said, forgetting everything she'd ever known about diplomacy and good manners, 'you're looking absolutely lovely with a very pronounced spring in your step. Have you got a new man?' she asked.

Mrs Khan smiled. 'Indeed not, Mrs Baxter,' she replied. 'But I have got a harp.'

SUMMER

THE MARQUEE

Mrs Khan was rather fond of her garden gnome, a decidedly fetching specimen with a spade for digging in one hand and a plant pot in the other. Whilst not as dapper as he'd been once, now that his paint was peeling and chips had appeared on his nose and cap, he was still a handsome devil. The boys had bought him for her when she and Mr Khan took them to the Gnome Sanctuary in their summer holiday from school. It was with a pang of sadness, then, that she saw him lying on the ground, his right arm next to him, severed at the shoulder. 'Can't be helped.' She said to herself. 'Accidents happen and he has suffered at the paws of Tigger on many occasions. He had good life.' She opened her front door, dumped her belongings on the hall table and made her way through to the lounge, a pretty room with picture windows overlooking the garden. She sat back on the sofa and kicked off her shoes. Before she could stop herself: 'That's better,' she announced to anyone who might be within earshot, of this world or elsewhere.

The day had been quite short but intense. Helena (as she now called herself, finally on stage in front of the paying public after years of daydreaming and thus wanting to be more than plain Helen) was keen to share her love of drama with the esteemed residents of Stackton-on-Sea. Dorothy had provided a selection of handmade chocolates with her most recently created fillings as well as some old favourites– all yummy – and Lawrence and Mrs Khan had provided the music. Truth be told, Helena wasn't without talent. She'd held the attention of the audience on her own for over an hour and a half. A full house – seventy seats – at ten quid a time had raised about five hundred pounds once the expenses had been taken care of. Not bad. And Helena had loved it. In fact, all the W.I. had loved it, as well as the holiday makers and locals wandering in to take shelter from the rain. 'After all,' thought Mrs Khan, 'Better to spend an afternoon in marquee being entertained than in B and B lounge drinking poor quality tea and wondering if weather is going to change before returning home.' At 11.15 that morning, they'd sold fifteen tickets – all to W.I. members – and were worried that it was going to make a loss, but no, courtesy of the English climate, all had gone well, one could even say swimmingly, given that this was a seaside town.

Dorothy's chocolates had practically soared unaided off the sales table. Moreover, she'd taken orders for another dozen or so boxes. If this continued, she'd have to get someone in to help. Maybe one of the other members would like to lend a hand, either for payment in luxury chocolate goods or a percentage of the profit. Personally, she didn't do it for the income but because she loved being a chocolatier. In addition, now that they'd finally starting selling them, their popularity was such that their sale raised considerable funds both for the local branch and whatever charity they were supporting at the time, so it was well worth the hours and energy she put in. She couldn't expect anyone else to work for nothing, though. Not everyone shared her passion for creating high quality confectionary.

***

Mrs Khan and Lawrence had had fun making the music that afternoon. They were used to playing this type of gig together now. They decided on the programme about an hour before lift-off and often did a fair amount of improvising. Each understood the other really well in musical terms, even though their personal contact was still rather stiff and formal. It wasn't that she didn't like him but that she felt more comfortable with other women since Mr Khan had passed on. Now that he was no longer around to act as a buffer, she was a little shy and never knew what to say. Sitting in her favourite armchair that evening, she mused 'Maybe my entry on W.I. Bucket List should be to find ways of feeling more comfortable with men. I had a husband for many years and still have two adult sons. It's not that they are a totally unknown quantity.' So thinking, she switched on the laptop and logged into her email account. Ah yes. There was an email from Gos and another from Amir. Popping a marigold cream into her mouth, she settled down to read their news.

On the way out of the performance tent, a tall man with long grey hair and a beard of similar appearance and proportions – a bit like a wizard, she thought – had told her 'the show was ace, ma'am, and the playing like a little bite of heaven come to earth.' The Stackton-on-Sea W.I. triumphs again!

**

A few streets away, Lally was getting worried. Del was coming home late more and more often these days. Sometimes he let her know but others, just didn't bother to turn up until way past the expected hour. She made up her mind to have it out with him. Chelsea was getting to be more of a handful than ever and was always asking for her dad. Lally liked the fact that they got on so well. She had friends whose children really didn't gel with their fathers at all. Indeed, not all of them knew who their fathers were. Some had even come out of test tubes and whilst she could see no reason to argue against such an arrangement, she found it hard to imagine what it would be like not knowing what the co-creator of your child looked like. She'd been lucky with Del, she knew, and didn't want to cause tension between them. But, she needed to know what was going on if they were going to find the means to fix it.

She gave Chelsea her supper and got her ready for bed. 'Where's daddy?' asked the little girl plaintively, a sad look covering her plump face. 'He'll be home soon, pet.' They sat on the settee together watching *Teletubbies* on iPlayer. 'I used to watch this with my own mum when I was small,' she told Chelsea. They'd viewed the original series together, although not on TV or even catch-up (which hadn't been invented then). Her mother had bought a set of DVDs and they'd sit together exactly like she and Chelsea were now, laughing and marvelling at the antics of the Tubbies and their Noonoo. She thought she probably loved it still more now she was an adult herself and could share it in the same way with her own child.

Del had never been this late and irritation was taking the place of concern. Chelsea would have to go to bed soon and wouldn't have had the chance to say goodnight to her much beloved dad. It wasn't fair of him to leave his daughter in the lurch like this.

Once Chelsea had settled down, Lally phoned Mrs Khan to ask about the afternoon show. She'd wanted to be there herself but what with her college course – practical days in hairdressers' at the moment – and sorting everything out at home, she couldn't make the time.

'We missed you,' said Mrs Khan, 'but it went well. Helena is building a fan base.'

As she put her phone down, it started to ring.

'Hi babes,' said Del. 'I'm not coming home.'

'What's happened? Where are you? Are you okay? Have you had an accident? Has the car broken down?' She asked.

'None of the above. I don't want to be married anymore. We'll sort everything out through a solicitor.' And the phone went dead.

TIME TO RELAX

Valerie (Baxter, as was; Ford, as is), now residing in the neighbouring borough – far posher than this one – wasn't finding it that easy to make the adjustments necessary for this marriage lark; not that she didn't love her husband and her unexpected change in circumstances. Getting home to find Lawrence waiting with a meal or a hug or, indeed, both; making joint decisions and plans (they'd booked to go on a five day taster cruise together later in the year); and snuggling up to someone at the end of the day – these were totally new and, well, utterly splendid experiences, ones she'd yearned for on many an occasion for most of her adult life. But, first there was the problem with accommodation. They were living in what had been Lawrence's house and she knew that was the right decision. He had all those harps to house, for a start, and the gardens were superb, much better than her own tiny plot, as pleasant as she'd made it. Another difficulty was that Winston the Third – so named because he was a third generation descendant of Winston the Great – and Professor Bodkin just weren't happy there, and they'd been her friends for a very long time. Hector and Billy didn't appear to mind as long as they still got their walks and treats but as we all know, dogs aren't as wedded to territory as cats are; and then, of course, there was the aquarium. Sea water aquaria take a lot more looking after than the freshwater variety and although the ladies of the W.I. were helping out – and doing an excellent job – they were new to it all and weren't doing it with as much love and skill as she could herself. She missed her house. That was the root of it. And if she was honest, she missed the single life.

Sitting in the elegant lounge of Lawrence's – whoops! – their house, she wondered if Mrs Khan was in and would like a visitor. She thought of Mrs Khan as one of those amiable, solid people who were good to have around. Self-contained, a little enigmatic and sparing with words, she could appear aloof, but that was far from the case. And she was wise. She'd been right about most things, especially 'the other stuff' or 'the private stuff' (as Val thought of it). It had come naturally enough after all, just like Mrs K said it would. Lawrence had been married before and anyway, he was a man, and 'it's different for them, isn't it?' thought Val, 'even in the twenty-first century.'

Everyone described Valerie Ford as out-going and vivacious, a description she'd done everything she possibly could to live up to, exaggerating her behaviour in an attempt to keep people at arm's length. Not that she didn't like them. Of course she did. But she liked her privacy, too, and didn't want to have to answer awkward questions about being 'Mrs' even though there'd never been a corresponding 'Mr'; and why she'd never taken the plunge. It'd become easier with the passing years. There were lots of widows when you got to her age and plenty of divorcees in her social circle but she didn't want to lie and was embarrassed about never even having had a boyfriend before Lawrence; and without Mrs Khan and her harp, even he would never have crossed her path.

Mrs Khan had been a loyal, astute friend and equally so when adopting the role of counsellor. When she picked up the phone, she was genuinely pleased to hear it was

Mrs Ford making the effort to call her and not a double glazing salesperson – not that she had anything against them doing their job, but the windows in her home were already exactly as she required them to be– or someone telling her that if she didn't complete her (non-existent) tax return pronto, she'd be cast in a dungeon and left to starve.

'Mrs Khan, it's me, Valerie. Lawrence is playing in a concert tonight and I'm feeling a bit restless. Are you up for a visitor?' Mrs Khan had been enjoying her quiet evening alone but recognised a friend in need. 'Of course, Mrs Ford. I shall put kettle on as soon as we terminate our conversation.'

Val smiled and got her jacket.

***

Lally sat in her favourite armchair deep in thought for several hours. Del's phone was switched off, so there was no chance of asking him why or what he expected her and Chelsea to do. Her first hurdle was to decide what to tell the poor little mite sleeping peacefully upstairs, oblivious to the explosion that had happened in her tiny world. Lally knew she'd have to share the news with her family and see if they had any ideas. Maybe there were bits of practical help they could offer but she couldn't face that yet. She could predict the comments and smug looks. They'd never liked Del and warned her against him from the start – 'he's all show and no substance, Eulalia,' her mother had told her, 'a bit like the produce from one of those home soda making machines. Sparkling on the outside but flat when you penetrate the surface' – but as neither her mother nor her sister had been particularly expert relationship-builders, she'd never seen any reason to listen to them. 'Maybe the entire human race – every single one of us – is total rubbish at relationships,' she thought, 'and it's not just my family and me at all.' It was a possibility that made her feel a little less lonely and not so much of a failure, in spite of not being at all sure that that was the case.

She knew she had no hope of sleep that night. So got the computer out and started looking up 'divorce'. How had it ever come to this?

***

Mrs Khan's coffee table had been beautifully laid out with Indian sweets – at least, that was what Val assumed them to be. She'd never been sure exactly of Mrs Khan's heritage and keen not to give offence, she didn't like to ask, even though she wanted to. She was fascinated by other people's histories, the more so if they appeared to be fundamentally different from her own.

There were bone china tea cups and saucers ('it's a long time since I've seen anyone use those,' she thought) and Mrs Khan had offered a choice of Ceylon Orange Pekoe or Assam tea; no coffee, in case it kept them awake. 'I wonder why it's not called Sri Lankan tea?' thought Val. She concluded without much conviction that the brand had been around a lot longer than the independent nation, so it might be too confusing to change the name. Maybe Mrs Khan's ancestors hailed from Sri Lanka? She made a note to look up the origins of the name 'Khan' when she returned home, but of course, she never got round to it.

'It will take you time to get used to it,' said Mrs Khan. 'It's a shock for everyone when we set out on this great adventure, and honeymoon days don't last forever.'

'I know, but I can't help thinking it might have been a mistake.' This was a shock even to Val herself, as she'd never even formulated the words in her own head before that instance. 'Maybe I'm too old to make such drastic changes after a lifetime of my own company and Lawrence was a single man for more than thirty years. It must be tough for him, too.' She said this with a sad note in her voice and a half-hearted attempt at a smile.

'I have perfect solution to your current somewhat dejected mood,' said Mrs Khan. 'Get your coat on. We are going calling.'

***

At Rainbow Cottage, the three women had warmed, tempered, stirred, mixed, blended, tested, drizzled and poured into moulds. They were now enjoying three mugs of rich, hot drinking chocolate. This had been an excellent idea. Val had completely forgotten her troubles. Mrs Khan was happy to be in the company of two such delightful people; and Dorothy was in her element. Dorothy secretly wondered if chocolate should be added to earth, fire, air and water. Surely it was equally important in the struggle to sustain life?

In spite of it being well past midnight when they made their way home, it was still warm and the rain had stopped a long time ago, so the walk back was a real pleasure. Val insisted on helping with the washing up and Mrs Khan insisted she took some sweets back to share with Lawrence.

'I'm a lucky woman,' thought Val, as she unlocked her door. Hector and Billy came running over to her, all waggy tails and excited whimpers. Winston and Bodkin looked up disdainfully and flopped back in their beds. As she walked into the lounge, Lawrence turned expectantly, a smile on his face displaying deep affection. He rose from the chair, walked over to her and wrapped her warmly in his arms. 'Yes,' she thought, 'this is definitely worth making the effort for.'

***

Meanwhile, back in his hotel room – Stackton Pavilion, a single night costing more than the typical week's holiday for the average member of the Stackton-on-Sea W.I. – The Wizard had been making phone calls and doing research on his laptop, a very posh job with all the extras available in the known world. The only thing it couldn't do was a *pasa doble*, and that was purely because The Wizard didn't know how to programme it in. He was going back home in a couple of days but his trip here had been illuminating and fun, not the dismal diet of mediocre music and dreary drama he'd braced himself for. The brass band had been exquisite and so diverse! The picture of such ensembles he'd had in his mind was one of very elderly white gentlemen with lowered lung capacity attempting to belt out Amazing Grace, but what he'd found was a highly polished ensemble of musicians ranging in age from sixteen to eighty, all experts on their instruments and able to tackle – successfully – pieces ranging from sophisticated arrangements of '60s pop right though Broadway musicals to what he thought of as serious classics. Amazing! And the WI! Where had they sprung from? Entertaining and engaging throughout and so talented! He picked another handmade chocolate from the delicious selection in the box and determined to continue his research in the morning. This hadn't been a waste of his time, after all.

***

When Dorothy picked up the phone next morning to find her caller was Mrs Khan, she was a little surprised. The two women got on fine, but there weren't usually any social connections between them beyond monthly meetings and the odd social get-togethers and workshop days with other members that took place in between the regular sessions. This was two days in a row and the previous evening had been unprecedented, albeit of great pleasure to all three participants.

'What can I do for you, Mrs Khan?' she asked politely.

'I trust you slept well?' enquired Mrs Khan.

'Yes, yes. Of course,' answered Dorothy, who didn't really go in for small talk. 'What can I do for you?' a little less patiently this time.

'I have been considering your desire to have your own entry on W.I. Bucket List.' Said Mrs Khan. 'I wonder, as you are unable to be in possession of your own plantation for the cultivation of chocolate beans, would it be satisfying to visit such a facility belonging to a third party?'

Dorothy stopped in her tracks. Rarely lost for words, she was experiencing that very phenomenon at that precise moment. Registering the silence, Mrs Khan continued 'Is everything alright, Miss Reynolds? Have I spoken when correct action would be to remain silent?'

Dorothy hastily regained her composure. 'Not at all, Mrs Khan. That is a wonderful idea. Thank you so much for thinking of me.'

The day was off to a much better start than either of the two women had imagined when they left the comfort of their beds that morning.

There was a lot to be said for breaking with convention and just getting on with it.

THE MEETING

'Okay, everyone. We all know why we're here today. There are plenty of refreshments at the side. Help yourself as and when. Who'd like to start?'

Val had called an extra meeting before the official start of the W.I. year. It was an exciting fixture – the Bucket List was going to be updated. Many of the wishes on the original had been fulfilled, so they were all keen to make their resolutions, albeit a good five months before New Year.

Everyone wanted to put their entry on the grid but, as usual, no-one wanted to be first. They'd all heard the news about Lally's breakup. Inevitably, the circumstances were variously related depending on the person reporting them. Mostly the response had been sympathetic and they were eager to help. But, she hadn't been seen for a while and before seats were taken and note books opened, Mrs Khan and Kathy had been elected to go round and see how she was getting on. Opinion was divided into two camps. The first:

'She should have fought for him. He's her husband, when all's said and done, and little Chelsea's father.'

Naturally, no-one could quite decide how this might have been put into practice but that was clearly beside the point. The alternative view was she'd made the right decision:

'Moving on and trying to get things sorted out without him is by far the better option. Much less hassle and heartbreak and more stable for Chelsea.'

There'd been no W.I. for a few weeks, so the women hadn't been together as a group but not seeing Lally in BestBuys or taking Chelsea out for walks was unusual. The W.I. members were concerned.

***

Back in her tiny garden flat, Helena was busy thinking about her next show. Maybe it should be a review, so some of the other W.I. members could have a turn at the limelight too. Or a two-hander, with Mrs Khan playing harp interludes. 'How much would it cost to hire the theatre?' she wondered. Probably too much to turn a profit but oh! How she longed to feel that stage under her feet! The entire membership could get involved, what with the need for costumes, programme sellers, refreshments, box office and all the other things involved. There was so much to do in these places and it'd be a great way to bring them all together in a single project.

But then she remembered. This was *her* dream. The Bucket List was long and there was no-one else on it who had aspirations to a life in the theatre.

***

'I'll go first,' said Maureen. 'My wish is quite simple. I want to go up to Stratford to see a show, have a really good meal and stay overnight. Maybe have a look round the town and buy a few souvenirs. I know it's not much but it's the sort of thing you want to share with someone.'

'Are you going to include "take members of the family with me"?' asked Kathy, 'or would you like one of us to come?' She sounded rather pedantic even to herself, but such details needed to be considered if the correct plans were to be put in place.

'None of the family has ever been interested,' replied Maureen. 'They all think it's too highbrow, although I don't know why. We've got theatres here and they go to them often enough. They even take trips to London two or three times a year. So, if anyone's interested, that's what I'd like to do.' The response from the floor gave the impression that there would be no shortage of takers when it came to appointing a companion or two. It was duly noted on the grid.

'I want to go Nessie hunting.' Said Beth.

'Better make it before the midgie season,' piped up Gloria. 'We went there once and I got bitten to bits. Or was it Loch Lomond? Anyway, it's notorious for people coming back in shreds covered in bites.'

After much persuasion, Mrs Khan had convinced Gloria that the W.I. would give her new interests and keep her mind away from worrying about her son. 'The members are good company,' Mrs Khan told her, 'and we have excellent, diverse programme of events.'

'I'm not keen on being with all those women,' Gloria had replied, 'but I'll give it a go. If it doesn't work out, I'll vote with m'feet.' They'd talked extensively about Gloria's 'problem boy' as she called him, and really, to Mrs Khan he seemed like a normal young man who'd grown up and away from his mother. Not unusual but also not always that easy to handle. Gloria had raised him alone after her husband died suddenly from a heart attack when Jamie was only eighteen months old. He'd been her entire life. Now a strapping thirty-two year old with a wife of his own, he was hardly a boy at all. But to Gloria, as to all mothers, no matter how old he might be, he was still her baby and she was finding it hard to let him go. 'What's the old saying?' Mrs Khan asked herself, 'A son is a son 'til he gets him a wife, a daughter's a daughter the whole of her life.' Well. Jamie had himself a wife now, so Gloria had to find different ways of living. This was her first meeting and Mrs Khan was hoping there would be many more.

Di (Dr Di, as the women called her to distinguish her from Di Lewis, the constable's wife) wanted to know if anyone would like to go on a narrow boat trip with her. 'What's always been the stumbling block is that there's no-one to share it with – ('This is beginning to be theme,' thought Mrs Khan). 'I'm not much bothered about where and when but I cling on to the hope that before my joints are too stiff to handle the rudder and get up and down the stairs, I'll have my pop on Britain's network of waterways.' Various women said they'd see what they could do but nothing was settled. But, Di had her own entry on the chart and no doubt in time, the appropriate arrangements would be in place, with or without companions from the WI. After that, all the women lost their inhibitions and the grid was filled up fast.

'Madam President,' said Kathy –

'Call me Val, please. You always have.'

'Right then. Val. As time's getting on, I suggest that we make a Bucket List Book, where members can leave comments about the wish list and either offer suggestions or let the person know that they'd like to take part in one – or several – of the activities. Or maybe help out with the arrangements. Some of these ideas are going to take a bit of organising and we could make it a community thing.'

'Good idea,' said Val, 'let's put it to the vote. All in favour, raise your hands.'

The meeting unanimously agreed and it was concluded that Kathy would buy a book and start heading up the pages.

'Thank you all for your time and input,' said Val. 'The next meeting, the first of our new W.I. year, will be here on 9th September and we have a wonderful speaker coming to us with a talk titled *The Bard's Naughty Bits: Swearing and Sex in Shakespeare.* There are programme cards on the table. Help yourself on the way out and see you in a couple of weeks.'

The members of the Stackton-on-Sea W.I. went home feeling excited and optimistic. They had a great deal to look forward to.

SENSITIVE ISSUES

'How lovely of you to call. Come in.' Lally stood aside so that Mrs Khan and Kathy could get through the narrow door into the hallway. 'How are you both doing?' she enquired.

'We're fine, love, but no-one's seen you for such a long while and well, you know, with the way things are, we wanted to be sure you were okay.' Kathy felt a little uncomfortable with this speech. It was like they were being nosey and had been gossiping behind her back.

'So you've heard then,' said Lally. 'Let me put the kettle on. Sit yourselves down.'

Chelsea was amusing herself on the floor with all sorts of new-fangled bits and pieces Kathy and Mrs Khan had never seen before, neither having young children in the house anymore nor grandchildren living close by. Apart from the odd glance and toothy smile, the little girl was quite content to continue playing with her toys. The room was comfortable and welcoming, rather crowded and messy but what could you expect with a three year old in the home?

By the time Lally returned with a tray laden with mugs, teapot, milk jug and biscuits, the two women had made themselves comfortable on the settee. 'Lovely upholstery,' thought Mrs Khan, who had always quite fancied the idea of working with soft furnishings. Then, 'I didn't realise young people still used teapots. I wonder what tea she favours.'

'I'd like to call him a vile scum bag and evil philanderer but the truth is, he was neither. At least, I don't think so. I've heard nothing from him or the solicitor he said he'd instruct, so I've got no way of knowing.'

'Was there no indication of the way things were going?' Kathy wanted to know.

'Well, looking back now, there were odd things; and then there were the nights when he was late home from work that should have made me think but you don't, do you, not when you're in the middle of it. And I was so busy with the hairdressing course and Chelsea, I suppose I didn't pay enough attention.'

'Interesting tea,' thought Mrs. Khan. 'I wonder what it is.'

'How are you for money?' asked Kathy.

'Oh, he transfers the house keeping into my account just like he did when he was living here, so I've got no problems there. And he pays half of the mortgage. I'm glad the house is in both our names. My mum and sister both said it showed that I didn't really trust him all along but honestly, we all know things aren't like they were fifty years ago!'

'What about your half of the mortgage?' asked Kathy. Mrs Khan felt that this line of questioning was a little too personal and shifted slightly in her seat.

'I've been in touch with the bank and we've arranged a plan. They've been really good. I don't know if I'll be able to carry on with the hairdressing, though, because child care is so expensive.'

'This is something we W.I. women can discuss, Mrs Evans. Don't give up your chance of a career because of this.' Said Mrs Khan. 'What tea are you using, if I may be so impertinent?'

'It's one I blend myself from a few others. I don't like many of the teas you buy in the supermarket, so I mix them together until it tastes right. I'm not very good at doing it a second time though, because I never write the proportions down. It makes it very hit and miss.'

'You've done extremely well. It is delicious and you have suggested something that I might in future try myself.'

***

As Lawrence and Val waited in the restaurant that evening, they were noticeably glimmering with contentment. When she got back from W.I. that afternoon, they'd had a quick cuddle – well, rather more than a quick cuddle, to be honest, but you don't want to know the details – and they were still bathing in the afterglow. He'd arranged for them to join a couple of his colleagues from the orchestra for a meal and they were in the Thai restaurant drinking a pre-meal glass of wine.

'Do you play anything?' asked Martin. He and his wife were both fiddle players in the Bristol Symphonic (affectionately known as Brasso), contemporaries of Lawrence and turning out to be very good company.

'Sadly not. I tried the piano when I was little but was completely useless, so it never came to anything.'

'Would you like to play something?' asked Miranda.

'Well, I've had the odd dream, but I'm no Mrs Khan and haven't got her talent or commitment. She practices for hours to get things right and she's streets ahead of me in every respect. I sing in the bath sometimes; and when we have a W.I. singalong, I enjoy myself a lot.'

'Have you thought of applying for the Brasso choir?'

asked Miranda.

'I'd have to be much better than I am,' replied Val. Lawrence pitched in at this point: 'I could help you learn some suitable songs for the audition and give you a hand learning the scores once you were in.'

'Wouldn't that give me an unfair advantage, a bit like nepotism?' said Val, secretly thinking as wonderful as it would be, she couldn't help feeling she was getting a bit out of her depth.

'I'm not going to do the audition for you, my love, just coach you a bit.' Lawrence's tone was so tender that Martin and Miranda both stared hard into their wine glasses.

Val thought of the grand piano in the music room – effectively camouflaged behind a wall of harps – and was very tempted. Besides, wasn't singing in a choir Gina's entry on the original list? She'd not fulfilled it yet. Maybe the two of them could have a go together. Now, that was an idea not to be dismissed too lightly.

***

Helena had been doing a lot of hard thinking around her subject. With Christmas on the horizon, surely there must be ways of putting on a W.I. show with everyone being involved. You don't need to be a theatre buff to enjoy getting on stage once in a while and she so wanted to share her passion with her friends. Most people liked to do something at that time of the year, even if for no other reason than to relieve the monotony. Possibly she could devise something they could do in that dead period between Christmas and New Year, when everyone got a bit fed up. She remembered her (much) older sister – now sadly deceased – telling her that when she was young, New Year wasn't even a bank holiday and people went back to work after Boxing Day and carried on until Easter. She often felt listless herself in those few days, sort of flat, after all the fun and excitement of the lead up to Christmas itself, so if she could create something with a focus, well, maybe that would work. They could use the W.I. Hall. That was always free during that dead phase and the stage was never used anyway. Not really. Just for the odd speaker when they got someone really special in and sold tickets.

She started creating an Ideas Chart, a bit like one of those pictures of sputniks and viruses and things, with a circle in the middle and lots of spikes leading out. She really believed she could get this to work.

***

In his log cabin in Heaven-Knows-Where, the Wizard was developing ideas of his own. Stackton-on-Sea had a grand theatre and he'd stumbled across a lot of talent in that short trip to Britland. He could really make something special from it all. 'Watch this space,' he said aloud as he closed his planner for the day. So doing, he rose from his chair and slipped out to spend the evening on the bank of the lake.

***

Over dinner, Mrs Khan pondered on how lucky she'd been during all the years of her marriage. Mr Khan had never given her any reason to feel insecure, not personally, financially or in terms of the stability of their relationship. She and the boys had wanted for nothing. She'd never felt there was any danger of things disintegrating and both Gos and Amir had turned out to be well-balanced, sensible men any mother could be truly proud of. She looked at the photos eminently displayed on the mantelpiece, ranging from the four of them as a family with the boys barely old enough to go to school right through to their own weddings with their beautiful wives. She wasn't so insensitive that she'd put their baby photos on public display. They were on the dressing table in her bedroom, where she could see them as soon as she woke in the morning and last thing at night before she dropped off into what was invariably an untroubled sleep.

She phoned Val to tell her about the meeting with Lally but there was no answer, so she'd try again in the morning. Surely with such a large number in the WI, child care could be sorted out. After all, Lally's hairdressing course had been on the Bucket List. It couldn't be allowed to flounder and fail.

STACKTON-ON-SEA WI
Programme 2021-2022

All meetings 2-4pm (unless stated otherwise) in the W.I. Hut

September 9th	<u>THE BARD'S NAUGHTY BITS</u> Swearing and sex in Shakespeare
September 16th 10am-4pm	<u>CARD MAKING WORKSHOP</u> *PLEASE BRING YOUR OWN LUNCH*
October 12th	<u>WHAT YOUR CAT DOES WHEN YOU'RE NOT LOOKING</u>
October 16th 10am-4pm	<u>CHRISTMAS CRAFTS WORKSHOP, INCLUDING UNUSUAL EVERGREEN WREATHS</u> *PLEASE BRING YOUR OWN LUNCH* *Donations towards material and use of hut*
November 9th	<u>STUFFING WORKSHOP</u>
November 28th 10am-4pm	<u>CHRISTMAS FAIR</u>
December 7th 1pm.	<u>CHRISTMAS LUNCH</u>
January 11th	<u>THE SERPENT AND THE SPHINX</u> Middle Eastern Dance, then and now

February 8th	GARDEN GNOMES: HISTORY, CULTURE AND ECOLOGICAL SIGNIFICANCE
March 8th	THE ART OF THE PERFUMIER
April 5th	THE GENETICS OF INHERITED ILLNESS
May 10th	LIFE IN THE ESTUARY The hidden world under the mud
May 14th 10am-4pm	CRAFT DAY FOR THE SUMMER FAIR *Please let the Committee know what you would like to make*
June 14th	GILBERT AND SULLIVAN, OR THE UNDOING OF THE MATURE WOMAN
July 2nd 10am-2pm	SUMMER FAIR IN THE MARQUEE

All other fixtures will be announced in monthly meetings and circulated via email. Please ensure we have your up-to-date email address.

PLEASE NOTE: *THE COMING YEAR LOOKS AS IF IT WILL BE PARTICULARLY BUSY AND INTERESTING, NOW THAT WE HAVE THE NEW W.I. BUCKET LIST IN PLACE. ANYONE INTERESTED IN EITHER ADDING TO OUR AMBITIONS OR TAKING PART IN ANY OF THE ACTIVITIES, PLEASE LET THE COMMITTEE KNOW IN THE USUAL WAY.*

SEPTEMBER

THE BARD'S NAUGHTY BITS
Swearing And Sex
In Shakespeare

'Thank you so much for that entertaining and informative presentation,' said Valerie. 'Shall we thank our speaker in the customary fashion?'

The members erupted in the biggest outpouring of appreciation ever witnessed in the Stackton W.I. Hut. Dorothy, bless her, had done her best to go along with it all but she was clearly a little uneasy and disappeared as fast as she could into the kitchen to make teas and coffees while the Q and A session was in progress.

Other members, though, wanted to follow up on all sorts.

'You said that his plays were designed to be crowd pleasers. How does that square with the need to keep the censor at arm's length?' asked Dr Di, the fourth or fifth supplementary question she'd managed to squeeze in. It was almost turning into a private conversation.

'Queen Elizabeth didn't appear to mind that much if her predecessors were shown to be less than perfect. In fact, she was probably in favour of it.' Andrew was enjoying his interactions with these women and didn't care how many questions he was asked. He went on: 'Shakespeare drew on histories that minutely documented the foibles and iniquities of the ruling classes, so he was only regurgitating what had already been written in detail by someone else. His contribution was to turn them into theatre.'

Before Dr Di could ask for further elaboration with a question relating, maybe, to King James, Valerie stepped in to give the next questioner a chance:

'In *The Merry Wives of Windsor*, when Caius talks about "making the turd" only he's meaning the third, is that why he made Caius a Frenchman, do you think, just so he could put that bit of double entendre in?' asked Flora, one of the members who only came to one or two meetings a year.

'We can't honestly know what his motivations were when he wrote these plays, beyond the fact that he wanted to be able to get bums on seats. Or possibly more likely, groundlings in the courtyard.'

And so the questioning continued. It had been a popular talk, in spite of the reservations of some members when it was mooted at the meeting of the Programming Committee.

Helena had been rooted to her own seat throughout, dreaming of the day when she'd be playing Ophelia, Cordelia, Constance, even Miranda, clearly oblivious to the fact that she was at least thirty years too old. Well, what's make up for?

***

Mrs Khan took out the packets of Assam and Ceylon teas (the latter itself a blend) and mixed them half and half. She then put a large W.I. spoonful (as the women had christened it – Dorothy had found it in a charity shop and it dispensed exactly the right number of leaves) – in the pot and poured on the boiling water. She hoped that Dorothy hadn't noticed her using bits and pieces from her own store cupboard to provide drinks for the meeting. She was fairly sure there was a Health and Safety rule against it but she wanted to try her ideas out with no-one knowing and wanting to flatter her efforts. She took a tentative sip.

'Not bad,' she decided. 'But plenty more options available before definitive blend.'

***

'So, how can we be sure that these things are accurate?'

Dr Di was still quizzing Andrew while he dug into his tea and biscuits. As she walked past, Val thought she might rescue him but he looked happy enough, so instead she went through to the main hall to help clear the last few chairs away.

'What did you think, Dorothy?' she asked.

'Better than I thought,' she replied, 'and the ladies loved it.'

'Dr Di certainly did. It started to feel as if I was playing gooseberry.' Val was only partially joking. 'Lawrence asked if he could come along but I wasn't sure how the meeting would react to a male interloper. I mean, I know the men can join now but we've never had any here, have we? Only to speak or entertain us. Maybe I'll invite Andrew to dinner with us one evening.'

Dorothy wished she could have the sort of confidence that would invite a complete – well, not quite complete – stranger to dinner. But then, did Valerie have the sort of confidence that would take her halfway round the world to work on a cocoa plantation? They'd never know. But then, they weren't really sure that Dorothy would.

***

'Season of mists and mellow fruitfulness,' thought Mrs Khan. Then, making her way along BestBuys fruit and vegetable aisle: 'I think he was right with respect to mists, but am not quite in agreement in the matter of seasonal bounty. Surely, if there is so much local produce at this time of year, things should get cheaper, not go up in price.' Given she was no economist, she didn't waste brain space putting too much thought into it.

She'd decided that when she went over to babysit Chelsea later that afternoon, she'd take her for a walk along the estuary. There was a section in the supermarket selling all manner of bird food, including big bags of what they called 'wild fowl pellets'. Luckily, they had two small ones left, so she put a bag in her trolley and continued with her shopping, throwing in a number of extremely exotic looking teas.

She'd considered (on many occasions) the possibility of turning a small part of her garden over to vegetables. She and Mr Khan had thought about it several times when he was still here with us but always concluded that they'd lose too much by way of flowers; and neither of them wanted to restrict the colourful display achieved nearly all year round. 'I wonder,' she thought, 'what could be planted that provides both food and beautiful blooms?' She'd read once that the Victorians grew runner beans for their blossom rather than to eat them, so maybe there were other plants offering equal advantages. She resolved to quiz both members of the WI, many of whom brought large trugs of excess produce to the meeting hut urging everyone to help themselves; and, of course, there were extremely helpful staff at the garden centre. She often thought that if she were young again, she'd quite like to work in a plant nursery, even if not in direct contact with the cultivation side of the business. But, Mrs Khan thought that the world was an infinitely fascinating place and not only did she have a great many things in mind that she would have liked to have the chance to pursue in greater depth, but she was never going to be young again, so the idea was never developed beyond the stage of playful fantasy. 'Most things start with a dream,' she thought, 'but not all dreams end with realisation of desire.' Besides, with everything else she was doing, she couldn't help thinking that twenty four hours in a day simply weren't enough.

***

'Foul mouthed and calumnious knave, thou art the most needless creature living!'

'Thy word is but the vain breath of a common man.'

'Yep,' she thought. 'I like the way this is going.'

Using only the material gathered from the W.I. talk, Helena was writing a play. It was fun, not just writing it but playing all the parts. Mind you, she'd only 'written' a couple of minutes' worth of dialogue so far but felt sure it was coming on well. Maybe this could be developed as something for the W.I. to perform to the paying public? Even at the Christmas show? 'Now, there's a thought.'

***

Back home in her small bedroom (currently doubling as a study) Dorothy was researching cocoa plantations. She knew it was going to be very hot, as cocoa beans would only grow within a thousand kilometres of the equator, which really isn't that vast an area, if you take into consideration the size of the globe. She found several in Indonesia, Africa and Malaysia, so it'd be a matter of choosing which of these countries she'd like to visit most and, of course, who would be willing to have her.

'It comes down to where they speak the most English I suppose,' she said to herself. 'I've always been so lazy about learning other languages. I can learn a bit. It'd be rude not to make the effort, but I'm never going to speak anything well enough in time to make myself understood.' This was going to take a lot of preparation if it was going to work. Still, Dorothy had the time and most definitely the inclination, so by this time next year, she was convinced her own dream would have been played out.

***

Mrs Khan put down her book and answered the phone.

'Good evening Mrs Ford.' Said Mrs Khan. 'How lovely to hear from you. Is there any way in which I can be of assistance?

On the other end, Val smiled to herself. 'Possibly, Mrs Khan,' she replied. 'Andrew – our speaker from this afternoon – has agreed to come to dinner at ours. We wondered if you'd like to join us.'

'That would be very lovely, Mrs Ford, but surely, Dr Di would be better in every respect than I could possibly be.'

Val hung up and marvelled anew at what an asset the branch had in Mrs Khan. So thinking, she flicked through her address book and pressed the link to Dr Di. This could be a very interesting evening.

NOT QUITE EAVESDROPPING

'And I got cut off, without him having a clue about what to do with the Cumberland sausage!'

Mrs Khan settled herself into a single seat for the bus journey home. She'd been to the W.I. Card Making Workshop and gone for a walk along the seafront before returning home for a quiet evening in front of the television. That nice man Mr Attenborough was on again tonight and there was so much to be learned from him. Besides, he was someone else for whom she secretly harboured the tiniest of soft spots, so she couldn't possibly miss out. She believed it to be safer to indulge the occasional mini-fantasy involving total strangers than to engage with the real thing at this time of life. As we know, Mrs Khan is usually a very wise woman.

The creation of beautiful cards was not an activity at which Mrs Khan felt herself to be especially talented. She'd been glued to the oil cloth, stabbed herself with scissors, painted the front of her blouse with gold leaf and inhaled several hundredweight of fairy dust. She felt she might be better employed making refreshments and keeping the hall tidy and clean, so made her way to the kitchen and got on with putting everything in place, while mulling over the possibility that we might no longer measure in hundredweights. The world was becoming a very confusing place.

Mrs Khan was not someone who habitually listened in to other people's conversations, but what should she do?

She could hardly turn and ask them to keep their voices down. That would obviously send the wrong message. So, having been party to only a small section of the dialogue, and finding it impossible to either close her ears or concentrate on her magazine – the Stackton-on-Sea W.I. News, issued four times a year courtesy of Kathy Borthwick and Shelagh Buchanan – she asked herself if it would be better to move to a different seat or to sit tight and do her best to concentrate on the beautiful scenery. Obviously, the former step would, again, send out the wrong signal, so she stayed where she was, giving herself the option of admiring the front gardens and hanging baskets along the route. At this time of the year, they were just starting to be past their best, so it would be a good idea to enjoy them while she still could. She felt quite relieved that at the present time, this was her biggest dilemma and found herself wishing that the same could be said for the whole of humanity.

***

Twenty nine women had attended the workshop that day, the highest number ever. The Stackton-on-Sea W.I. were well known in the county for producing wonderful craft work for their Christmas fair and Dorothy's chocolates had become a living legend.

Cards were just one of the crafty delights on offer. They also made wreaths, decorations, unusual gifts, bouquets garnis for mulled cider, dried herbs and all sorts of smelly things to put in drawers and cupboards – the list goes on. It goes without saying that the women of this particular branch were extremely talented and generous with both their time and energy.

The September workshop for cards and decorations, followed by Unusual Evergreen Wreaths in late October and 'stuffing' in November were a staple of the W.I. calendar. This last was always popular, giving the women the opportunity to create their own perfumed bags of great delicacy and exquisite perfume. What little was left over at the end of the fair was stored for the following year, with the exception of the little gauze packages filled with herbs and dried flowers, which were duly delivered to the hospice to be distributed among the patients or sold in the shop. Either way, they were always gratefully received.

***

There was a particularly loud guffaw from the seat behind. It was clearly something that only the two women in question were able to understand, because Mrs Khan really couldn't see the funny side. 'Is it a cultural thing?' she wondered. Probably not. She'd never had difficulty seeing the humorous ramifications of a good story in the past, so believed this explanation to be unlikely. It must have been one of those situations where you had to be present to appreciate the comic implications, definitely. Much against her better judgement, she was starting to be drawn in and had given up even making the effort to distract herself.

***

The workshops offered a welcome chance to socialise as well as create lovely things. In addition to the Stackton women, members of other W.I. branches in the area were invited and there were always some who pitched up to learn some of the skills being offered in return for a small donation towards materials, tea and biscuits. They either brought their own lunch or went out to one of the many seaside cafes littered around the town. It was a very popular day.

Mrs Khan was a great believer in community and being part of it. She was also a great believer in recycling and with the exception of glues – environmentally friendly, of course – and threads for sewing, the materials provided for the creation of these artefacts were recycled waste collected by the members over the course of the year. It ensured that the handiwork was truly unique and could in its turn be recycled. However, not for the first time and much to her regret, she reminded herself with a tinge of sadness (while still trying to remove the gold leaf from her clothing) that this type of activity was something at which she did not, and could not, excel.

However, for her role as Refreshment Officer she felt considerably better equipped to deal with whatever the day might bring and had thrown herself into it with great relish.

Lally, on the other hand, had a wonderful time. Chelsea had made a total of seven cards, all adorned with elves (so it was rumoured) and copious thumb and finger prints in varying colours and definition. Not content with making cards, she found the decoration of her face an equally satisfying outlet for her talent; and even made the odd attempt to use her skills to enhance Lally's natural beauty. She was clearly a child with artistic leanings. Or maybe not.

For the first time ever, Jenny was showing the members how to do iris folding.

'This is what the finished article looks like,' she said, holding up a number of cards in succession. The members were genuinely impressed.

'Will we really be able to produce something like that in a few hours?'

'You'll surprise yourself,' said Jenny and offered them a large number of different templates to choose from.

'How did you cut out the designs?'

'Drew them in first and then used a Stanley knife to remove the solid parts, It'll be much clearer once you get going.' Jenny knew that sharp knives in the hall were not a good idea. She knew from past years it wasn't just Lally who brought her daughter, it was popular with other children, too – 'I wonder why we never see sons' thought Mrs Khan – who made an unusual array of cards, not necessarily recognisable as being pertinent to the Christmas season but always popular and no doubt received with great delight by grandparents, uncles and aunts.

The new member recruited that day, Bryony, was much closer to Lally's age than most of the women and had two daughters, one two-and-a-half and the other five. Of course, there was Di Lewis but she was very self-contained and had no children. She was like one of those Blithe Spirits, who came and went almost unnoticed unless you were tuned into them. They'd all been surprised when she'd asked for an entry on the Bucket List, but it was inserted on the grid and although a Sports Day wasn't going to be the easiest thing to get underway, they'd do their best and no doubt come out on top.

Mrs Khan hoped that Bryony and Lally wold be company for each other. It was good to have such a wide age range in the branch and they all got on well and learned from each other; 'But still,' thought Mrs Khan, it would be nice for them to have someone at similar stage of life.' As Lally was the only member with such a young child, Mrs Khan often wondered if she felt a bit lost. Three year olds were grandchildren for most of the women and whilst totally adored, were another generation distant, so only a certain amount of empathic understanding was possible. 'The world is so much changed,' she thought. 'Much of it is unrecognisable. What do my generation have to offer young people now, apart from a friendly face and a refuge in times of need'? Sobering words indeed.

***

In one last effort to shut out the conversation being held behind her, Mrs Khan planned her forthcoming morning with Chelsea. She'd arranged to take her out the next day, so that there'd be time for Lally to visit her family and try to sort out some sort of help without Chelsea overhearing or requiring too much attention. Mrs K had decided on a visit to the pond on the Green, where they could feed the ducks the excellent wild fowl pellets again and watch them playing. Far nicer than telling Chelsea they were squabbling. 'Do they have duck ponds in America?' she mused. Surely they must. But, she'd ask one of the boys when she emailed that evening. Her regular trips to the Green were an essential part of Mrs Khan's weekly routine and she'd struck up an acquaintance with most of the local dog walkers and the other visitors out enjoying the air and the wildlife. Stackton-on-Sea was, to be sure, such a friendly, hospitable place.

***

But her quest to mind her own business was hopeless. Their voices were getting louder, the laughter more raucous and Mrs Khan had run out of topics to engage her brain. She was almost sorry when the bus pulled up at her stop and she was obliged to leave behind the unfolding drama. She glanced at the seat to her rear as she moved to the exit and was surprised to see that they looked nothing like the images she'd created for them in her mind's eye.

'Ah well,' she thought, hanging up her bag on the stand in the hall. 'I can only hope their conversation provided them with as much entertainment as it did me.'

She got out her laptop and opened her account. Ah yes. There was an email from Amir. 'I suppose Gos must be too busy at work,' she thought. 'Or maybe service is down.' Still she had plenty to say to Amir. Time to make enquiries about ducks.

THE CALL OF THE WILD

As Lally walked up the beach, she was not best pleased to see the seat where she'd left her clothes was now occupied by a young(ish) man. To be fair, there were very few benches along the seafront and there was none other with any free space, so she accepted it with good grace. He had as much right to be there as she had herself, after all.

Once she was again fully clothed and drinking from her flask of tea, he glanced up and spoke to her.

'Enjoying the first of the autumn sunshine?' he asked.

'The water's still warm,' she answered, in a neutral sort of tone. No need to be unpleasant. It wasn't his fault there were too few places to sit and he'd been very discreet. He turned back to his magazine.

'Are you here on holiday?' she asked. He was visibly surprised at her interest but not displeased. 'I'm visiting, yes. Are you?' he asked.

'No. I was born and bred here.' She thought better of expanding, particularly as regards to speaking of a young daughter, secretly regretting it was a sad indictment of the age that such revelations could be unwise.

'It's a lovely place.' He offered.

'Do you visit often?'

'Not often enough,' he replied. 'But we all lead busy lives.'

Lally gathered up her things and left him to his magazine.

***

Along the estuary, Chelsea was prancing around like a young pony.

'Oh for the energy of the young,' thought Mrs Khan. They'd been joined by Beth walking her dog, a sweet cockapoo called Sam. Sam's enthusiasm easily matched that of Chelsea.

'What's the next thing for you, Mrs K?' she wanted to know.

'I think I have my hands full as it is. The harp needs much attention, as do garden and house. Enough for me to help in quests of others. And how about your own aspirations?'

'Oh, I'm not as brave as you are, Mrs K. I know it probably seems a very simple thing to you, but for me, well, I'm not used to doing things without the involvement of my family and it might be a pipe dream. They all think I'm mad to want to go to Scotland looking for a monster that almost certainly isn't there.'

'A metaphor for life,' thought Mrs Khan, and then offered 'Better not to find a non-existent monster than to find a non-existent monster' she replied. 'But jury is still out on Nessie. Do not give up your dream.'

***

At the Ford residence, plans were being made. 'Do you think I should stick to traditional English fare or have a go at Italian or Caribbean?' asked Val.

'I'd stick with something simple, my love. It's possible Andrew does a lot of Caribbean cookery himself and almost certainly far better than you or I can.'

'And what do you think about asking Mrs Khan as well as Dr Di? I know it'll give us an uneven number but I don't want him to think he's being set up.'

'I can ask one of the boys in the band if they'd like to join us. That'd even up the numbers, but do we really need to? It's the twenty first century, after all.'

In the event, there was no need, as when Mrs Khan got back home, she found Gos sitting on the sofa. After all the necessary greetings and endearments, Mrs Khan asked what he was doing here and why he hadn't let her know he was coming.

'I took a place on a conference in Bristol at the very last moment. I thought I'd give you a surprise.'

When the invitation for Val and Lawrence's dinner party was extended a second time and Mrs Khan politely declined because her son was visiting, Valerie immediately insisted that Gos should come too. 'The more the merrier,' she said, 'and we'd love to meet your son.'

So the date was noted on the calendar and Mrs Khan settled down for an evening of catching up with events on the other side of the Atlantic through the medium of an email from her eldest son, Amir.

***

Lally was both grateful and pleased that the W.I. members had rallied round to help with Chelsea. Her own family had found themselves far too busy and thought in any case that she should be "fighting" for Del to return. 'Who could blame him for going off,' her mother had asked her, 'when you spend all your time learning hairdressing or messing around with the WI? Much good it did you studying psychology in the sixth form. They should have taught you how to keep a man.' Pondering over the sad fact that she and her mother would never understand each other, she put Chelsea to bed and opened the computer, looking for local solicitors specialising in divorce. 'No time to let the grass grow under my feet,' she thought. 'Time for action.' So saying, she noted down a couple of phone numbers and resolved to start making inquiries the following morning. After all, it was something that had to be done at some point, so she'd set the ball rolling. The sooner the process with its associated pain was over, the better it would be all round.

**

Mrs Khan was naturally thrilled to have Gos at home again, even for a few days. She was no fool, however, and couldn't help wondering why he'd suddenly taken a place at a conference that normally he'd have decided on weeks before and more importantly, why was Ren not with him? Renate Khan wasn't particularly keen on her husband's English home but usually accompanied him on these short trips, if for no other reason than it gave her the chance to see how her own company was performing in outlets over here. She was itching to ask but didn't dare. 'Ask no questions, get told no lies,' she decided. She'd find out soon enough.

Her email to Amir that evening was gently probing and, she hoped, would encourage him to share information with him without appearing to be interfering.

'Good evening Amir (*she'd never get used to the time difference*)

How are you and your lovely family today? I had wonderful surprise this afternoon. Your little brother has appeared with no warning. No Ren, either. He is here for a conference, he says, but hasn't given me any notice of

how long conference will last or why decision so sudden. I am hoping all is well.

Do take care, Your loving mother.'

Amir, however, wasn't quite that daft:

'Hi Mum. Sorry, Gos has said nothing to me. He must be okay, or else we'd have heard something. Make sure you feed him well. Don't want Ren to think you've neglected him when he gets back.'

'Ah. Well, in that case I have to be patient.'

She resisted the temptation to tuck him up in bed, limiting her inquiries to questioning him as to whether or not he would like her to wake up and make him breakfast.

'S'alright mum. I have the alarm on my phone and can grab a bite on the way. I'll probably be on my way to the station before you're up.'

Right, she thought. Definitely being told tactfully to keep nose out of younger son's business.

Her night's sleep wasn't quite as peaceful as it usually was. 'Things can only get better,' she promised herself, and willed herself into the arms of Morpheus.

OCTOBER

WHAT YOUR CAT DOES WHEN YOU'RE NOT LOOKING

'So Tigger isn't giving me unconditional love when he rubs himself round my legs at all,' thought Mrs Khan. 'And it's clear now why he was so unresponsive to Gos.'

'Good meeting, Mum?'

Her heart gave a little leap at hearing her son's voice from the kitchen. 'Excellent, as ever.'

***

'This is extremely kind of you, Valerie, and you too, Lawrence.' Andrew had come armed with a bottle of brandy, but, he explained, (keen not to embarrass them) they shouldn't feel he was being over-generous, because it had been left over from a get together at his place and he wanted it to have a good home.

'Thank you so much,' said Lawrence, taking Andrew's coat. 'We're all here except for Dr Di. Come through to the lounge while we're waiting.'

Andrew was fascinated by (what seemed to him) the enormous harp standing in the corner of the room and when Lawrence took him through to the music room, he was totally incapable of speech. All that changed, however, when Dr Di arrived, the meal got under way and the conversation started flowing along with the wine.

'Well, Gos, lovely to meet you. Mrs Khan says you're here for a conference.' Said Valerie.

'Yes and no. I also came to test out the idea of a job at Bristol Temple Meads University.'

Mrs Khan had to work hard not to choke on her orange juice. This was something he'd not yet shared.

'How lovely.' Said Dr Di. 'May I ask what post you're interested in?'

Gos told them and explained as best he could in simple terms the nature of the research he'd be undertaking. Dr Di clearly understood what he was talking about, as she did a lot of questioning, but as for the rest of them – well, let's just say they're not scientists.

'This meal is delicious,' said Andrew, feeling that the conversation was becoming a little too esoteric. 'Was the cooking a joint venture or is the kitchen ruled by one of you alone?' he asked.

'We planned together but Val did the cooking.'

'Only because Lawrence has been busy with rehearsals. Preparing for this evening was fun and I'm hoping it'll be the first of many.'

'My place next time,' said Dr Di. No-one disagreed.

Mrs Khan and Lawrence entertained the assembled company with an impromptu harp recital when they'd all eaten their fill. Gos, of course, had never heard his mother play but knew of her long-buried desire. He sat there marvelling at the skill and obvious love with which her fingers flew across the strings and was deeply moved that this was his mother and that she had followed her desire at long last. She'd done her best to ensure that he and Amir had also followed theirs. 'All starts with a dream, boys,' she used to tell them and they'd both been lucky enough to see their hopes turn into reality.

Mother and son were quiet, content and hopeful on the walk home. This new twist in the life of Mrs Khan hadn't even been on her private wish list, let alone that of the WI. She did wonder though, what had brought it about. Only time would reveal the working of her son's mind. As much as she wanted to know, she knew better than to pry.

***

The Christmas Crafts workshop was another of those occasions when Mrs Khan wished she were not quite so woefully inadequate. The Unusual Evergreen Wreaths, when made by someone else, were beautiful. Felt-covered cardboard rings were the base for stuffed cloth birds and mistletoe, linen flowers and handmade foliage fashioned from wire; others were adorned with homemade holly, ivy, Christmas bells and robins; still others purely abstract, some looking like circular clematis and others a simple jumble of colour and texture. In Mrs Khan's hands, however, they were more like the inside of a particularly badly fitting dustbin lid.

The decorations were equally exciting. Garlands of handmade flowers, the materials used ranging from photocopied music manuscript right through to brightly coloured crepe paper. Angels and fairies sprung up on the tables from assorted cereal boxes and fabrics, all having previously had a normal life span in the homes of the members and their families. There were many other artefacts produced by the women, all highly imaginative and each, in its own way, a thing of beauty crafted with love.

The day flew by, albeit with Mrs Khan spending most of it providing drinks and cakes for the participants, admiring the products of their toil as she handed out the refreshments. 'Ah well,' she thought, 'at least I have talent to keep teapot topped up. We must make what we can of what we have.'

This year they should raise a healthy amount for their annual charity – the *Let's Share Allotment*, a project for under-privileged children from the local region, teaching them cultivation skills and providing them with their own home grown food. Their W.I. offering should make a significant contribution to its continuation for the next few months.

***

Gos was pretty sure that that was Tigger disappearing through an alien cat flap. But no, it couldn't be. He had a comfortable, loving home and wouldn't need to go elsewhere for love and – more importantly – bowls of cat treats. 'Still,' he thought, 'I've got a comfortable loving home myself and it didn't stop me.' Finding this train of thought rather uneasy, he nipped into the chip shop and got a fish supper for himself and chips and pickled onions for his mother.

Sure enough, Tigger reappeared looking considerably more full of food – stuffed, really – with a smug look on his face. Things only got worse when he sauntered up to another front door and slipped his way in.

'Ah well, boy, you've got one up on me,' he thought.

***

'So, what will you do if Ren definitely will not return to England?' asked Mrs Khan over dinner. 'I don't know, mum. Things haven't been going well for a while. I think Ren would prefer a man a little less tied up in his work.'

Not knowing what to say, Mrs Khan said nothing, but continued to eat her chips. At least he was letting her hear the uncertain meanderings of his mind, although she did wonder if it might have been better had he kept them to himself. If he decided to come alone, well, it would be wonderful to have him close but she'd worry about his marriage and the two grandchildren. If he decided against the job, her hopes would have been built up only to be dashed; and so the thinking continued with every single permutation of Gos's possible decision being examined for good and bad consequences. 'Definitely better had he not said anything,' thought Mrs Khan, 'for me, at least. I'm passed being able to weather sleepless nights.' With that unwelcome thought taking up space in her head, she snuggled down under the duvet and very quickly nodded off into a peaceful night, dreaming of nothing more taxing than the Christmas fair.

The next morning, she started to wonder if she should put one of those collars on Tigger, the ones with the little canisters where you can put notes inside. He was looking so plump these days. He surely couldn't be putting on all that weight just from what she fed him. She put his food bowl down and its contents disappeared faster than the Apollo rockets had reached escape velocity and he quickly made his escape through the cat flat. Well, the speaker had informed them that cats often visit several different homes on their daily wanderings. She'd pop into the pet shop and see what she could find. Time for a canine diet, she decided.

Having made that decision, she settled down for her own breakfast and wondered what the coming day might bring. The only thing that was certain was that it wouldn't be another surprise as delightful as the arrival of Gos.

TIME TO SING

'ah ah ah ah ah ah'

'Good, good. Try not to put an 'h' between the sounds.'

'aa aa aa aa aa aa' – this was easier said than done.

'Better, much better. Now, don't forget to breathe down into your abdomen and let it out evenly as you make the sounds.'

Lawrence was no singing teacher. Indeed, he was no singer either but he had had half a dozen lessons forty or so years ago (probably more. A lot more.) and was vaguely aware of how singers warmed up, having seen lots of choir trainers taking their members through their paces. He was teaching Val a couple of songs for her sing at the audition for the Brasso Choir and she wasn't doing too badly at all. Gina was going to join them this morning but hadn't arrived yet, so Val and Lawrence were playing around on their own. He'd asked one of his colleagues for advice on repertoire. Her husband was a member of an opera company – he couldn't remember which one – and did a lot of freelance work. He would know far better than Lawrence what songs would be best for the inexperienced, untrained chanteuse; and he'd also been to the choir mistress to ask about the audition process and what she was looking for when she tried out potential new members.

'They need to blend in with the sound. No need to have a wonderful voice,' she'd explained. 'No need to have any training. Just a love of singing and music. It's hard work and can be tiring when we do concentrated rehearsals in the lead up to a big concert, but it's fulfilling. Tell your wife to apply. She'll love it.'

As neither Val nor Gina had a clue what voice they might be, he'd got hold of a couple of songs slap bang in the middle of the range and decided that Rose, the choir mistress, could allocate them to the appropriate section. To Lawrence, it was an arcane process that whilst he admired, he had no real insight into. He'd wondered if it had been wise to offer to help, thinking that maybe he should have found a singing teacher for Valerie and her friend but felt sure that neither of them would have felt confident enough to go to an expert. They were, as Val kept telling him, keen to sing *not* to join him in the profession.

***

Lally was finding it tough fitting everything in but was determined not to abandon her hairdressing course. She'd been able to organise a nursery place for most of the time she was at lectures or the salon; and although there was a rumour that Stackton-on-Sea College was hoping to open a crèche, it seemed unlikely it would be open in time for her to benefit from it. During the time Chelsea wasn't at nursery, the women from the W.I. had organised a babysitting rota and were giving Chelsea a wonderful time. She knew she'd be struggling soon for money though, as childcare was a big financial outlay, in spite of all the support she was getting.

She still hadn't heard anything official from Del. Indeed, she'd heard nothing unofficial either. His phone was still switched off and she was starting to think he'd probably got a new one.

'Get in touch with his family, Eulalia,' said her mother. 'He can't just abandon you and Chelsea. You were always too soft. A pushover. I'm not surprised he left you. He's a spirited man. He needs someone with a bit of oomph.'

'Thanks, mum,' said Lally, again considering it to be poor taste to remind her mother that her own husband had left her for a woman twenty years his junior when she still had two young daughters for whom she was responsible. At least Dolly – Dorabella (where did her parents get these names from? Lally often wondered.) seemed to have a stable relationship. Not married. Dolly couldn't see the point. 'It always goes to the bad,' she'd said, when Lally asked her why she never wanted to take the plunge. 'Cheaper not to have to pay for a divorce.' And she was probably right, thought Lally, sitting with Chelsea on the settee that evening. 'Am I getting cynical?' she asked herself. 'I hope not.'

***

Back at the Ford household, Val and Lawrence were pondering over their matchmaking skills.

'Well,' asked Lawrence. 'How do you think it went the other night?'

'I've heard nothing and the next W.I. meeting isn't for weeks. They seemed to get on okay though.'

'We'll just have to keep our eyes and ears open,' said Lawrence. 'Now, do you want to go over that song again?'

***

Lally bumped into Helena in the college refectory. 'Canteen, back in my day' thought Helena. They were at the same college, Helena studying performing arts rather than hairdressing. She was brushing up her '*Shakespeare's Insults*' dialogue and wondering if she could write a play utilising all the themes from the WI's programme for the year. She liked the idea of using this month's lecture title for the play and building something to show the world what a fantastic time they all had. She was starting to think it might be better to concentrate on writing rather than performing but whenever she remembered that beautiful feeling of stepping on stage in front of an audience, she knew she could never give up on that side of her life.

'So what do you think, Lally?' she asked over her second cup of cappuccino (oat milk, of course).

'Well, it sounds like a lovely thing to do. It might well bring everyone together in a single project and as you say, there are so many different things involved in putting on a show, no-one has to feel pressurised into doing something they don't want to.'

'So, are you going to be taking part?' asked Helena.

'I don't know. Nothing in my life is clear at the moment.'

'But you'd be interested in principle, surely.' Helena was doing her best not to be pushy but was so enthusiastic herself, she found it difficult to understand that anyone else could be reluctant.

'I don't want to mislead you. First there's the hairdressing business. I'll be starting up on my own soon and want to give this venture my very best shot. Then there's Chelsea. Childcare takes up so much of my money and time. I can't afford to take on anything that might mean I can't buy food and pay the electric bill or that could take me away from spending time with my own daughter.' Lally was a little put out by Helena's insistent questioning. It was okay for her. She was on her own now and couldn't be expected to understand the pressures involved in bringing up a child single-handed.

'But you could bring her with you.' Said Helena.

'I really think you should consult the entire branch about this. If you want them all involved, you need to include them in your thinking from the start.'

It wasn't quite the response Helena had been hoping for but at least it wasn't an out-and-out 'no'. She'd mention it to Mrs K next time she saw her. She'd have the right touch to galvanise the women into action if anyone did.

***

Keen not to intrude on her son's privacy, Mrs Khan suddenly found that there were many plants needing attention in the autumn garden and the shed held all manner of pressing jobs screaming out to be attended to. The house was a standard sort of semi – and making phone calls without being overheard was a bit of a challenge.

The conference had finished a few days ago but Gos was giving himself time to refamiliarise himself with the town where he grew up. He was also trying to unravel all the conflicting streams of thought bouncing around in his skull. He just wished that Ren had come with him. After all, the children were as good as grown up now and Gos Jnr was away at college. They could easily be left on their own with supervision from friends. He also wished he hadn't seen that gorgeous mermaid emerging from the waves the day he arrived. Where was she now? He wondered. Maybe better to put such thoughts to one side. Things were complicated enough.

CHOCOLATE, CATS AND COCOA BEANS

Dorothy had considered getting herself a cat on many an occasion. The local rescue centre was always looking for good homes and when she saw those pretty little faces pleading to be taken in, it wasn't easy to resist. She'd have to defer the decision for a while, though, as her research into cocoa bean plantations was encouraging her to think she could be spending a significant time away from home during the coming year. Besides, in the run up to Christmas, she'd have lots of chocolates to make and still no-one to help her, so she couldn't take on anything new yet, even an undemanding four-legged friend.

***

Somewhere in the middle of Who-Knows-Where, the Wizard was consulting his diary. He really ought to arrange another visit to Stackton-on-Sea before making any big decisions. What he'd seen and heard was truly amazing, the moreso because it had been in an insignificant little seaside town in the UK of all places; but it could have been a fluke. Better not to be hasty. 'That's what I'll do,' he thought. 'These backwaters always put on Christmas shows. I'll spend the season there and see what they come up with.'

So thinking, he set to organising the rest of his year.

***

She'd whittled the possibilities down to three: Guyana, Trinidad and Tobago; and Sri Lanka. At first, she'd fancied Cameroon. She'd loved the name since she read those books by Gerald Durrell when she was a girl, but then discarded it. Too out of the way and an unknown quantity too far. Sri Lanka was very low on the list of cocoa-producing countries (although not as low as Guyana) but it sounded such an interesting place. And didn't they film that programme about the hospital there? The one that was supposed to be India? It looked lovely. And she knew they had elephants. But there was unrest again and she wasn't sure she could handle being mixed up in all that. The other two countries were safer in her own mind, not just because of what she thought of as 'the difficult situation in Sri Lanka' but because she was fairly sure that the mixture of French and English would see her through. At least she was making progress.

But before that, she needed to make plans for the Christmas Fair. 'I really must do something about finding an assistant. Nothing's going to happen if I don't make it clear I need help.' With that thought in mind, she drafted an advert to go on the board. She'd get Val to mention it at the next meeting, too. If no-one was interested, all her energy would be needed to provide enough for her usual stall. Not putting her best foot forward would certainly not do at all.

***

'Mrs Fisher,' called Mrs Khan over the hedge, 'how about joining me for a cuppa and a piece of cake?' It was clear to Mrs Khan that Gloria was again fretting over her son. Her shoulders were hunched and she was attacking the pruning with a vigour that couldn't be healthy, for either the plants or Gloria herself.

'All right then,' replied Gloria somewhat ungraciously and by the time she'd made her way round to Mrs Khan's garden, the table was laid with a variety of homemade cakes and a pot of tea, this one a blend of Darjeeling and Nilgiri. 'A bit of a waste, really, seeing it's so difficult to get hold of now,' thought Mrs K. Still, in the interests of the Science of Tea Blending, it had to be tried.

'She's pregnant now, and instead of coming to me for help, they're going to her mother all the time or the child-birth place, you know the one, that dodgy centre run by volunteers over by the park,'

'Ah yes,' replied Mrs Khan. 'Must be a proud moment for you, the first grandchild.' She thought it best to stay as neutral as she could manage.

'But he's still a baby himself, Mrs Khan!' 'Good Grief!' thought Mrs K. 'Six foot four and weighing about hundred kilos? I'm glad no baby of mine came into the world that size!' She wondered if she should have converted the height to metres or centimetres but realised she was straying from the matter in hand.

'True, Mrs Fisher. We mothers always think our children remain preserved in a time long ago when they needed our constant supervision and guidance on how to live life. But sadly, that is not how it works. They grow up too, just like we did, and need to make their own mistakes.' Oh how simple it all sounded!

'But they go to her, the mother-in-law,' wailed Gloria, clearly upset. Mrs Khan was thinking this wasn't the best blend she'd come up with but again brought her attention back to Gloria's obvious distress.

'Women often find it easier to go to their own mothers than someone else's. This is not rejection of you but rec-ognition that life for Jamie is now independent, decisions have to be made by couple and each half of couple has equal say. And, of course, equal rights.'

Gloria sat silent staring at her tea. 'I wonder if I should go and get a pot of something a little more tasty,' thought Mrs Khan, but decided that it wasn't the tea that was causing the despondency and lack of interest in her visitor, so stayed put.

'Mrs Fisher, I will try to be honest without offending. I know it is difficult. I have two sons myself, both of whom grew up, married and emigrated to United States. It's hard. But it is now their life and they must make of it what they will.'

'But how? How, Mrs Khan? What can I do to make it better?'

'Probably nothing in short term,' replied Mrs Khan, unwilling to tell any porkies. 'But it gets to be less of a problem with passage of time. When you see what an excellent job Jamie and his wife do with their new child, you will be proud that you raised such a fine, independent boy.' As Gloria said nothing, Mrs Khan continued: 'I tell you what, Mrs Fisher. Why do you not get a little more involved with WI? There are plenty of different activities on offer and many ladies there have had same experience. They can provide support and suggest ways in which they found it helped to move forward for themselves.'

'But all this Bucket List stuff! There's nothing I want to do.' Said Gloria.

'Well then, Mrs Fisher, maybe we could make your entry onto the list "*Find something interesting to be involved with*". No need to have specific aim at present. Let time sort it out for you.'

Gloria went home a little less anxious whilst remaining unconvinced.

***

Mrs Khan washed up the tea things wondering what it must be like to have no other focus in life but a son who was finding his own way in the world, very successfully, but without the need to remain tied by the invisible umbilical cord that Gloria found so hard to sever. She threw the remains of the tea onto one of the flower beds. 'Unsuccessful blend and a waste of good Nilgiri,' she thought. How privileged she felt to have no worries greater than the sparsity of a particular type of tea. 'Ah yes,' she thought, 'life has treated me well.' And mulling that thought over with memories of years well spent, she started to prepare the evening meal.

NOVEMBER

WEBS

Just outside her front door, Mrs Khan stood totally transfixed. The rain was cold, it's true, and her bones were
beginning to dissolve but standing watching this tiny little
animal making its web in her ivy was beyond anything
she could have imagined. She followed its progress as it
moved round and round, laying down more threads in a
beautiful, delicate pattern that was made the more lovely
by the reflection of the sun off the droplets of rain. When
the assembly was complete, its maker disappeared into the
foliage – to rest, so Mrs Khan hoped, rather than to lie in
wait for its prey – and all that was evident of its existence
was this wonderful testament to the diligence and deter-
mination of life itself. 'Better than trying unsuccessfully
to meditate,' thought Mrs Khan, turning back through
her front door to change her wet clothes and dry her hair.

Gos was definitely going back to the US for Christmas.
She'd miss him but always knew that his stay here was
only temporary. She wondered how he was getting on
with his book but as with everything else, she didn't like to
ask, although she did ask him to keep her updated on his
progress. 'If he wants me to know details, he'll share them
with me,' she thought, at the same time hoping he wouldn't
expect her to read it. 'Too clever for me,' she decided, 'and
not really my thing.' He'd told her how much he loved it
here, that he hoped Ren would return with him so he could
take up the post at the University he so wanted and that

they could make this their permanent home. She thought it unlikely but as ever, kept silent on the subject. 'Ren has never been keen on our eccentricities,' she observed silently. At least, she considered them eccentricities herself. Amir would probably say that they were all classified in one of those big books he had in his office and were eminently treatable. 'Is life really more complicated now than it used to be?' thought Mrs Khan. 'Or is it like policeman, not getting younger at all but seeming to just the same?'

Gos and Lally's budding friendship was something she was really pleased to observe. It was nice for both of them to have company and as they were each missing a spouse, albeit (Mrs Khan hoped) for different reasons, they could understand each other better than many others would. 'Oh what a tangled web we weave,' she thought, remembering the delicate structure she'd seen built that morning. 'No tangles there. Maybe better if human doings had a little less brain and a little more heart,' she decided.

***

While Val and Lawrence were both attempting (with little success) to get some sleep, Mrs Khan was sitting in her back garden stroking a sleeping Tigger, gently snoring on her lap. 'Not many more nights like this one before next spring,' she told him. 'Clear, crisp, every star in sky visible.' It was completely still and the air, whilst cool, was comfortable and smelt of the sea. The waves could be heard breaking on the sand in the distance, although the sound was only just audible. In spite of the darkness, she could clearly see the outlines of her beloved plants and almost felt their greenness. It's true that nights spent like this were more frequent in summer and if the weather turned, as it inevitably must, she'd stop indoors and keep to the comfort of her bed, but 'All the more reason to enjoy it while we can, eh Tigger?' Tigger twitched a little but didn't bother to answer. 'Both getting old, boy, so more important than ever to look after ourselves.' This was greeted with a sigh and a stretch.

Gos saw the two of them sitting there from his bedroom window, quietly luxuriating in the night air. 'Shall I go and join them?' but no, best to leave them to it.

***

Val and Lawrence were restless for different reasons, Val because she was finding everything a bit much at the moment; Lawrence because he wasn't at all sure he was giving either Val or Gina the best chance of getting through the audition for the Brasso Choir. Val's life prior to becoming Mrs Ford had been sedate and easily managed. Now, apart from the difficulties involved in keeping two households in good nick, she had less free time due to the full-time presence of a significant other in her days and weeks – wonderful but time-consuming. There was the pressure she'd put herself under with the upcoming attempt to enter the world of the choral singer and then, of course, there was the volunteering she'd started a couple of years back for the Wildlife Trust; and it goes without saying, there was also the WI. Something had to go – but what?

***

The Christmas Fair was almost upon them, and then there'd be the Carol concert. Such a busy time of year and everyone panicking and buying too much and regretting it once the bills came in. The meeting that afternoon had been longer than usual, what with all the extra bits and pieces they were offering this year. The cupboards were bursting and it was going to be difficult to shift the lot on a single day. Still, the Stackton W.I. was well known for its excellent fairs and they were hopeful.

What had surprised them all was that Di (the constable's wife) had turned up with several dozen Christmas tree decorations, all created with her own fair hand – fairies of the most exquisite delicacy, choirboys looking exactly like they were going to burst into song, angels that could easily be flying and taking care of their charges. They were all crafted from wire and different fabrics and would fetch a good price. No-one had had any idea she had such a talent, or in fact, anything about her at all. They'd all made the assumption that she worked, and that was why she shot off so promptly at the end of the meeting but now they couldn't be so sure. For her part, Di figured that if the W.I. were going to help her with her Bucket List entry, she'd have to try to give something back. It was a good deal on both sides.

Dorothy had made a new range of chocolates just for the upcoming market and she'd succeeded – just – to get them all packaged beautifully. 'Still able to produce the goods,' she said to herself, never seriously doubting she could. She'd been most surprised to be approached by that new woman, Mrs Khan's neighbour, about helping out with the manufacture. 'I'll give you a trial,' she said, and a date was fixed.

The Bucket List had been forgotten in the turmoil that surrounded the winter festivities. Still, they were doing okay and were well on track to achieve it all by the end of the W.I. season. Kathy had started to look for a Spanish class and after Beth's success with the adorable Sam – a gorgeous animal rescued as a result of the first Bucket List – she was also going to get a dog. Moira's hair now had stripes of green, blue, magenta and orange. A bit of an acquired taste, perhaps, but it was her entry on the list and she'd achieved it. Her husband had been enthusiastic and her daughters had been aghast. Well, the saying is, as we know, that you can't win 'em all. One out of three had to be a decent enough result.

AUDITION PIECES

Anyone who's ever done an audition will know they're not always much fun. Some people look at them as an opportunity to show off (me, for instance). Other people are indifferent, a sort of 'what the hell' mentality and others still are terrified.

Val was one of the last. Poor Lawrence was doing everything he could to reassure her that it would be totally fine. She knew the pieces extremely well, sang them like she'd been born singing them and would definitely not make a total fool of herself, which was her principle concern. What he didn't tell her was that the choir mistress had said that if she could sing in tune, hold the melody and didn't sound like a warthog, there was a place for her.

Gina was of the 'what the hell?' mentality. 'Honestly Val,' she said, 'all I wanted was to sing in a choir, a Can't Sing Choir at that. If they don't want me then so what? There are always places to go for a warble if you're brave enough to do it and now Lawrence has helped me, I think I have that bravado.'

In the event, Val not only discovered she was a high soprano – Gina was a high alto – but that they'd both be an asset to the Brasso Choir. They celebrated by going to one of the many restaurants – Mexican for them this evening – both of them forgetting to let their respective spouses know that they'd be home late. At least neither of the men thought it worth informing the local constabulary.

They'd joined in the rehearsal and were a little concerned that they wouldn't be able to live up to the commitment required, let alone reach the standard but, as Gina said, 'She thinks we're okay. All we need to do is our best.'

Lawrence bit back 'I told you so,' when Val eventually got home and informed him that she was now a member of the choir attached to his orchestra. He'd hoped she'd call and when she hadn't, had worried that maybe something had gone wrong. He was pleased for her and also for himself, not to say relieved that he'd done an adequate job in coaching them. The choir and orchestra went on tour together from time to time and there was every chance they'd get the opportunity to travel together. He'd love that and was sure she would too.

She showed him the pile of music she'd been issued and he promised if there were any problems, he'd help her. 'Gina, too, if she gets stuck.' This was going to be fun.

Gil, on the other hand, was unimpressed. 'What do you want to sing in a choir for anyway?' he asked. 'What do you want to play darts for?' was the only reply Gina could come up with on the spur of the moment.

'That's different,' he informed her. 'Oh of course it is,' she replied. 'Anything you want to do is automatically considered to be more important than anything I want.' This wasn't going well. However, she was determined to stand her ground.

Gil threw his magazine down – something to do with motor bike racing – and stamped up the stairs to bed. 'He's not going to spoil it for me,' she promised herself and hoped that she was right.

Rose was pleased. Two new women, both with lovely voices, both musical and enthusiastic. 'Shame we can't find a few more men,' she said, uttering the same lament of choir trainers up and down the country. She packed up her things and made her way home.

***

The afternoon had been beautiful, one of those interludes you only get during autumn, crisp and bright, the light having that mystical quality associated with the coming of winter. The sea had been sparkly and inviting, belying the fact that it was almost certainly too cold at this time of year to venture in and swim.

Gos had taken the afternoon off rather than work on his book. His intention was to watch the waves and try to sort out what to do about his future. It had been a real stroke of luck getting this sabbatical – most of his colleagues had had to write their magnum opuses alongside a full teaching and research schedule. He liked this place. It was a bit difficult living with his mother, of course. Not that she wasn't the perfect hostess and a truly lovely mum but an adult son or daughter used to living away from home, in Gos's case on another continent, well, it's never ideal, is it.

He wondered what they were up to now back in West Virginia. Gos Jnr was probably burning the candle at both ends studying and living the high life, Cher (not his choice of name) getting ready for her final exams before going on to college and Ren – who knew what she might be up to? She spent a lot of time working away all over the US and often further afield. She'd easily get work here, if he could convince her it would be the thing they needed to refresh their marriage.

He sat on the bench thinking of nothing very much, watching the sun go down and enjoying the sunset.

'What a mess,' he told himself, then put the thought aside and waited for the sun to disappear totally for the day before making his way home.

***

Mrs Khan had spent the day making sweets. She'd take something out of the freezer for their supper. She was playing simple tunes on the harp when she heard the door open.

'Hi mum. Get your coat on. I'm taking us out to dinner.'

Not being someone who needed to be asked twice, she did as she was told and enjoyed her evening meal twice as much for it being unexpected and not having had to cook it.

***

Val's head was way too buzzy for her to be able to sleep. She'd have to go the chemist and get some of those herbal pills she'd heard people talking about if this insomnia was going to be a regular occurrence.

She went downstairs to make a milky drink and when the armchair deliberately put itself in her way so that she stumbled over it and stubbed her toe, she was pleasantly surprised to discover that she could hop perfectly adequately on one foot without even the need to swear to help her balance. Hector and Billy looked unimpressed and neither cat was anywhere to be seen.

Through the window, she could see the full moon perfectly framed between the now bare branches of the oak tree at the bottom of the garden. She thought of Lawrence sleeping peacefully upstairs; and marvelled at the change in fortune that his entering her life had brought. Yep, it was quite true that there were still teething problems but nothing they couldn't handle.

In the comfort of the marital bed, Lawrence turned over and pondered on something very similar. 'Nothing could ever have prepared me for this,' he thought. 'Shall I go and join Val or leave her to her thoughts?' He thought it wise to give her the space to focus on whatever she needed to and hoped that she was as happy as he was himself. This was something he really didn't want to lose.

MARKET DAY

'Three thousand, two hundred and sixty nine pounds, twenty seven pence.'

Gina had totted up the takings. It had gone well, no doubt about it. There was more here than they'd ever made. A lot more.

For many of them, the most important thing about the fair was that it concentrated the mind. Only four weeks to go now and for those who celebrated in the traditional manner – too much food, too much to drink and too many rows – there was a lot to be done. After all the effort expended making the Christmas market successful, a lot more energy had to be generated to repeat it all in glorious technicolour in the comfort of their own homes. Why do we do it?

***

Helena's Christmas show was a very low key affair. Mrs Khan had said thanks but no thanks to the request to do some of the reading. Andrew, on the other hand, after his roaring success with *The Bard's Naughty Bits* had been very happy to step in. Was there something going on between him and Dr Di? Difficult to say but fingers crossed. Chelsea was dressing up as an angel and reciting a 'poem' (more of a statement, really) she was learning at pre-school. That, at least, was the plan.

In the event, Chelsea was a little restricted by the costume. It meant she had to stay clean and that really wasn't her idea of a good time. When Lally finally caught up with her, she had cake and buttercream all over her face and the angel wings had migrated to her front, meaning that they, too, had their fair share of sticky, sugary adornments. The skirt, which she'd tried to keep intact, had been doused in orange squash. 'I can still do it,' she informed Lally. 'We'll ask Helena what she thinks,' was her mother's reply.

The audience didn't seem to care that it was less than perfect but Helena noticed that odd man with the white hair and beard. He didn't look happy. Maybe he wasn't child-centred and didn't realise how difficult it can be to drill them in finer points of the performing arts. Lally felt that Chelsea was probably more likely to become a naturalist than an actor but who could say? She wasn't quite four yet.

***

The process of clearing up was always the longest part of the day, or so it felt. When the last piece of litter had been allocated to the appropriate bin, the last tea cup washed and returned to the cupboard, the last table folded up and returned to the side room, there was a sense of achievement almost on the scale the first chaps must have felt when they sunk the flag in at the top of Everest.

Mrs Khan was packing up her harp and was again glad that Gos was around to get it home for her. 'How do you manage with this, mum? It weighs as much as a fully grown man.' Not quite, maybe, but she could see what he meant. 'Did you ever think of taking up the penny whistle instead?'

***

'Here's to us all and here's to the W.I. Bucket List.'

Mrs Khan, Lally, Val and Lawrence, Helena, Gina and Gil had all accepted Gos's invitation for a pre-Christmas dinner, as he'd be away on the day. They'd opted for a Chinese meal. Dorothy had chosen to babysit Chelsea, more because she didn't want to have to socialise with such a large group than because she wanted to spend the evening with the little girl but whatever the reason, everyone was okay with her decision and she enjoyed her choice, as did her ward.

The food was delicious, the company well-chosen and cohesive; and the conversation uncontroversial. The only one who didn't seem totally comfortable was Gil, but even he loosened up in the end, being surprisingly receptive to Lawrence's *Anecdotes of a Jobbing Musician*. Gos was an excellent host and he, too, was able to thaw some of the ice in Gil's demeanour without any apparent effort at all.

'So,' he wanted to know, 'what do you think of Gina's singing?' he asked.

As even he could hardly say he was totally against it, he praised her efforts and hoped that it went well for her. Val gave them an update on the coming season's concerts and Lawrence sang the praises of Mrs Khan's progress on the harp.

They were all thoroughly relaxed by the time they made their way home and the news of the success of their fundraising efforts was a good omen for times to come.

***

'Are you looking forward to Christmas, mum?'

Mrs Khan was doing the final tidying up for the night and getting Tigger's food ready. She was thrilled. Everyone liked Gos and who doesn't love it when their children are popular?

'It's always nice. It's good to have a day when nothing happens and everything is closed. The world is too frantic, even for people like me whose time belongs to no-one but ourselves.'

'You'd be welcome to come to the US with me, you know. You haven't seen Ren and the kids for years.'

'Better for you to go alone,' replied Mrs Khan. 'Things for you to sort out, with you wanting to move family to Stackton.'

Didn't he know it.

DECEMBER

CAROLS AND CAKES

'Sing out, everyone. Give out your joy,' commanded Jack, throwing his arms around with great abandon and doing his best to get the women to deliver a command performance. 'It's the season of goodwill we're celebrating not mourning the loss of the Titanic.'

This was everything Val hated, even though it was a way of indulging her new found love of singing. Gina didn't seem to mind, so to Val's way of thinking, a fifty percent success rate was better than a zero percent success rate. To Lawrence it was just another date – one for the mortgage, as they used to call it, even though he was giving his services free. To Mrs Khan – well, it wasn't her favourite thing but at least people were trying to be happy.

Dorothy was still smarting over the Christmas Fair. She'd sold all her wonderful chocolates and been given so much praise it had been embarrassing; but ever since that awful man who looked like he'd stepped out of *The Lord of the Rings* suggested she should sell him all her cherished recipes so that he could build a factory and they could be made commercially ("Stackton Choxies; the real thing") she'd been poised like a panther ready to spring. He was actually suggesting she give up making them altogether and with it, her rights to do so, so she could 'enjoy old age without the hassle of standing all day in a kitchen. It couldn't be much good for her varicose veins'. She was hopping mad, no matter how much damage that might do to her varicose veins. 'Miss Reynolds finds chocolate business highly satisfying. She does it not for financial gain but for love and fulfilment.' Dorothy had been grateful to Mrs Khan for stepping in – she couldn't be sure she wouldn't slap him with whatever came to hand – but annoyed because she hadn't found the wherewithal to stick up for herself. She could be 'a consultant' he said, if she still wanted a hand in it all and they'd credit her on the wrappers. Insufferable man.

So, as we can see, this wasn't kicking off to be the best Christmas Stackton-on-Sea had ever played host to.

***

Gos had already left for the USA to share Christmas with his American family. He definitely wanted to move back to this lovely little town with its picturesque seashore and gentle, kindly people. He knew convincing Ren wasn't going to be easy, particularly since the little indiscretion with the research assistant but he intended to give it everything in his repertoire. Mrs Khan had done her very best not to overhear the telephone calls. It was clear all was not well.

***

'Tidings of com-fort and joy, comfort and joy,
    O-oh ti-dings of com-fort and joy.'
'Go for it, ladies! Don't be shy!' Jack was truly heroic in his attempts to get them to sing.
'Go and find another W.I. branch to torture,' thought Val.
Lawrence kept winking at her. It was making it more

fun to join in and the two harpists accompanying so beautifully made it almost a pleasure, with the emphasis most definitely on the 'almost' and not the 'pleasure'. In the past, it had been Kathy's husband on an electronic keyboard and he'd done his best, truly he had. Still, he was glad he hadn't been called on to do so again. He was enjoying an afternoon watching the racing and eating pork pies. 'Each to his own,' thought Kathy, handing round the Christmas cake – shop bought this year, as every single homemade cake had gone at the fair and there'd been no time to make any more.

***

'Miss Reynolds. What are you going to do for Christmas?' asked Mrs K.

'Oh, what I always do. I have a lazy day indoors.'

'Would you like to come and have lunch with me? It won't be traditional English. This is not something which I can claim to do well. But I would be honoured if you would be present at my table.' Dorothy was surprised and pleased to be asked. 'Could I have time to think about it?' she said, not being someone who broke easily with tradition. 'By all means. Take all the time you wish.'

***

The Wizard couldn't understand these people at all. The summer show had been a revelation but this Carol Concert and that offering at the fair were, well, not exactly a shambles but they lacked the polish he'd expected. And that chocolate woman! Anyone would have thought he'd made an indelicate proposal instead of trying to secure her a safe and comfortable future.

He hoped the other seasonal entertainments would be better and, of course, there was the 'traditional Christmas offering' at Stackton Theatre. Maybe that would restore his faith. He'd come a long way and didn't want to go back home disappointed.

***

Christmas Day was a pleasant enough event that year in Stackton. Val and Lawrence had been invited to have lunch with Martin and Miranda and pitched up with a bottle of the best champagne they could find. Lally had (reluctantly) gone with Chelsea to her mother, who made sure she missed no opportunity to remind Lally that she'd been a terrible wife and that the most dire problems lay ahead for Chelsea, growing up – as she now was – fatherless – 'Not really, mum, she still has a father. He's just made himself scarce,' was the only rejoinder Lally could come up with. Why couldn't her mother leave it alone just for one day? she pondered, wondering when they could reasonably leave and get back home. Mrs Khan had prepared a three course meal for herself, Dorothy and Gloria, who'd declined the opportunity to go to Jamie's in-laws and although she joined the other two women, her heart wasn't in it. Dorothy took with her a big box of chocolates she'd kept back from the Christmas Fair. She and Mrs Khan ended lunch by choosing one each, and Gloria went back home as soon as she could. The rest of the W.I. members did all the things they usually did and whilst most of them were as happy as we hope to be on this happiest of festivals, there were some who would be glad when life got back to normal again.

***

The New Year traditionally offers promise for all but who could say where it would lead? Mostly, it would be much the same as ever but for some, real changes were afoot.

Mrs Khan, sensible in this as in most things, made the same resolution as she always did: 'To Create Happy Memories'. After all, she didn't smoke, wasn't overweight or in need of a gym membership, kept in touch with everyone she wanted to and needed no urging to practice the harp.

'Goodbye Old Year,' she thought, giving Tigger his last meal of the day. 'Tomorrow will be another day to enjoy and treasure.' She made her way up to bed and hoped that for once, the midnight revelries wouldn't wake her. In the event, it was Amir phoning her with greetings for the times ahead that disturbed her sleep. 'No mum, I haven't heard anything from Gos and Ren except best wishes for the season. Really, I think you should stop worrying,' he told her, unconvinced that his words would do the trick. But he needn't have been concerned, for as soon as she put the phone down, she dropped off to sleep again, waking to a miserable looking morning that she hoped was not a portent of the things to come.

JANUARY

GOODBYE APRIL COTTAGE?

'You don't have to do this, you know.' Lawrence wasn't entirely sure that this was the right time to choose what he felt to be a rather drastic option.

'I do. I'm living in Bayfield now with you, my husband. I don't need to keep this house on. Apart from all the financial outlay, there's the problem of the day to day running of the place. The aquarium alone needs more intense care than I can give it and it's not fair to ask the W.I. to carry on tending it forever.'

'Bayfield's only ten minutes' walk away,' – *a little optimistic maybe, thought Lawrence* – 'and there must be companies who could transport the aquarium to Bayfield. Between us we can manage.'

They were having another look round Valerie's house, having bid farewell to the estate agent who they'd asked to value it. 'This will go in a flash,' she'd said. 'Well maintained, good size, low maintenance back garden. The front can be concreted over for a car' – *oh no! Not my lovely spring flowers! Thought Valerie* – two minutes walk to the sea, decent shops. Great for someone wanting to commute to Bristol, as it's not that far to the station. Oh yes, we won't have this on the books for long.'

Valerie wanted to cry but didn't. She couldn't understand exactly where her reluctance was springing from. It wasn't a spur of the moment decision and she and Lawrence had talked about it a lot.

'At least get another agent in,' said Lawrence. 'A second opinion never hurts, no matter what the situation.'

'It's not the price she quoted that's bothering me,' snapped Valerie, surprising herself with her own forcefulness.

'Well leave it for a bit. There's no hurry. Or you could rent it out, see how you feel about someone other than you living here.'

'Are you suggesting that I might need it again at some point?' asked Valerie.

Lawrence, with his new caring persona, was starting to think it might be best to keep his mouth shut but as she'd asked the question: 'Well, we don't know what's going to happen. Men usually die a bit younger than women' – *should I have said that? he wondered*– 'and it might be too painful to stay in the marital home' – *was that the right things to say?* – 'or we might find over time we're just not compatible.' *Oh good grief! That's hardly going to smooth things over, you stupid oaf! When you're in a hole, you fool, stop digging!* Lawrence didn't think he'd get any prizes at Charm School for this current contribution to his wife's dilemma.

'Well, if that's how you feel,' declared Valerie, suspecting that there was smoke billowing from her nostrils. She turned on her heel and flounced out, leaving him standing there wondering why he hadn't trusted his instinct and stayed silent. Very much wanting to chase after her, he used a bit of his newfound diplomacy and figured that this might be the moment to let her have her own time and space.

***

'Mr Ford is speaking sense,' said Mrs Khan. 'Far from being insensitive pig, he is trying to understand why you should be so insistent on parting with home you have enjoyed for many years. He wants to prevent anything that might bring regret.' Mrs Khan wasn't at all sure she was helping matters but was doing what she could.

'I can't believe he'd say those things. I'm a married woman now. He should be supporting me.'

'Poor man is making every effort to do just that,' thought Mrs Khan, but didn't give voice to this opinion.

'I've changed,' said Valerie.

'Indeed you have,' thought Mrs Khan. 'Instead of being dog rose, strong, determined and indomitable you are Cecilia Brunner, fragrant, vibrant and – dare I even think – feminine.' She'd noticed the change in Lawrence, too. No longer the brusque, famously irascible curmudgeon, there was a more pliable quality to him. In their personal dealings, he was more yielding and in his harp playing he was less like an effervescent firework display and more like a gentle, caressing paramour. 'Still early days, Mrs Ford,' she said out loud. 'And different challenges in mature years. When twenty, one doesn't know who one is or how to live one's life and has to work it out through medium of another human being. Not easy. But in sixties, life choices have been made. Personality accepted even if not understood and adaptations made in the way one conducts one's everyday existence. Instead of two people growing together, more like parallel lines with bridges between to come together in centre.'

Valerie was calming down. Maybe she'd been a little abrupt in her reaction.

'May I suggest you have another jalebi?' asked Mrs Khan. Valerie smiled and settled down to a pleasant chat with her good friend.

***

'We've just been asked to value a beautiful cottage in Barretts Avenue. It's not even on the market yet.'

The Wizard sprung to attention as if poked in the backside by a piece of electrified wire. 'Can I see it?'

'We'll have to talk to the vendor. She's not given us the instruction yet, so we can't take you in without her permission.' More to the point, she thought, without the key.

'Do that for me, please,' replied the Wizard and put the phone down, a self-satisfied smile spreading across his face. Yes, this was all going his way.

NEIGHBOURS

'I'm so nervous. The only time I've ever hosted anything this big was with the W.I. and there were loads of people involved in the organisation.' Val had taken Mrs Khan's advice and invited all their neighbours in to say hello and enjoy a bit of post-Christmas conviviality. 'It might make you feel as little more like part of your community,' she'd said. 'A little less like the New Girl or someone passing through. Not quite as drastic as selling former home.' To some of them, it would be the first time they'd met the intriguing new woman in Bayfield, who'd had such an impact on their hitherto somewhat irascible neighbour.

Lawrence had given up trying to reassure her. 'Let her discover for herself that as long as there's enough food and drink on these occasions, all is perceived to be well,' he thought. He was almost right.

***

Grumfuttocks was in full flow by the time he made it as far as Val's car door. She found out much later than the name conferred upon him by her in a fit of pique should have been Gruntfuttocks, but she couldn't even remember where she'd heard it, let alone the correct spelling and pronunciation.

Have you heard that saying about our pigeon siblings? Arguing with an idiot is like playing chess with one of them? No matter how good you are, the bird is going to shit on the board and strut around like it won anyway. I don't know where it came from – neither did Val – but it seemed to her it applied in this case; and thank you for it, if it's your creation.

Mr G lived next door to Lawrence – to both of them now. He'd inherited his beautiful house a few years earlier and had done it justice. At least, the outside and gardens were beautiful. No-one had ever seen inside. Val had tried to be friendly but without getting very far.

He was what might diplomatically be considered a difficult person, albeit very pleasant to Val – or what he considered to be pleasant, which isn't necessarily the same thing – but had some sort of downer on Lawrence. Lawrence, for his part, had always tried to be neutral, as he was only too aware of his own past reputation as snappy and over-sensitive. He felt he was hardly in a position to make judgements on his fellow man. Or woman.

Before his retirement, Graham had run one of the laboratories at the local hospital and believed that put him on a level above everyone else, certainly above a mere musician who swanned around the world having a good time faffing around 'like an adolescent girl' – his words, not mine – with a harp. 'He doesn't talk to me,' he informed Val. 'He's rude. I say hello and he just waves and goes inside. And when he sits in the garden in the evenings, sometimes you can hear his music.' He'd waylaid her coming out of the front gate on the way to the supermarket and was giving it to her straight, as he saw it.

'He's a man of very few words,' said Val. 'He doesn't talk to me much, either. But if you feel as if neighbourly relations aren't good, maybe we could all get together one evening for a meal and see if we can have some quality time together.'

'Oh no,' he said. 'He invited me in a few times and the food was terrible. He got takeaways in. How bad mannered!'

'Well, maybe a coffee then, or afternoon tea?'

'I don't have time for that. I've got all my DIY to do' – *ah, that must be the endless noise from next door, she thought* – 'and the dog needs walking. You should know that. You have dogs yourself and one of them a greyhound into the bargain, so you appreciate what it's like having to give them enough exercise.'

'Well, greyhounds are couch potatoes. They need to walk, of course they do, but unless they're racing, they need a couple of short walks a day and they're happy. Maybe we could all go out with the dogs and stop off in a café somewhere?'

'Sorry Valerie, but he's been rude to me. He leaves the windows open when he's practicing so you can hear him all over the neighbourhood' – *unlikely, thought Val, but if it really is the case, well, most people have to pay to listen to that. Shouldn't you be grateful?* 'He ignores me and doesn't take me into consideration' – *really? It's usually your car parked across our frontage, not the other way around* – 'and made no attempt to include me in anything ever since I moved in.'

'Okay. If that's how you feel. It's a shame not to get on with neighbours, but if you'd prefer to keep away from us, fair enough.'

'Valerie, my good woman, *purleeezze!* I have nothing against you but I don't like bad behaviour, so want nothing to do with him.'

'That's your right. But the fact is we come as a package,' *that's a turn up for the book, she thought, bringing herself up with a start. It's certainly news to me* – 'so if you want cordial relations with me, you have to have them with him, too.'

Since that exchange, Grumfuttocks had made a point of ignoring both of them. He'd cross over the road if he saw either of them walking towards him, wouldn't answer the door if they'd taken a parcel in for him so it had to be left on the doorstep, turned his back if they were in the road at the same time. A great pity but his choice. What can you do?

She saw him storming up the path and could hear his footsteps banging in the passageway.

'What now?' She thought.

She'd asked Lawrence some time ago if he knew what had happened to cause such a rift.

'We got on okay when he first moved in. Everyone in the Close did their best to welcome him and all was well. Then during a particularly windy night, my bin was blown over and all the recycling waste ended up in his front garden. I went next door to pick it up but hadn't asked him first if it was okay. He came out and told me it was bad manners not to check if "trespassing on his property" was acceptable and that had I been more responsible, the rubbish would have ended up in my garden, not his.' Val had raised her eyebrows at this but kept quiet. There must be logic in it somewhere, if only one knew where to look. 'I apologised and thought things were fine. Then, a few of us got together for an evening meal. It was a lovely evening and we sat outside chatting and laughing. I hadn't invited him. I hadn't deliberately snubbed him but we'd had several evenings together previously and it didn't occur to me to ask him to join us. He knocked on the door the next day to complain about the noise and since then, he's either found cause for complaint or ignored me altogether. I gather he's the same with everyone, so I stopped trying to smooth things over.'

A great shame, but if that was Mr G's preference, Val could do nothing but accept it. Lawrence's response was virtually a speech, so she knew the conflict must affect him quite deeply. She'd always been very lucky with her neighbours. They'd all rubbed along together and she missed them sometimes, the more so because relations with next door were strained.

It all came to a head during this New Year celebration, set up – as we've seen – by Val and Lawrence to bring the community closer together. Everyone in the road was invited– including Mr G – as well as some of their friends. Mrs Khan, not a party-goer by nature, had declined, but several other W.I. members were there, with about a dozen residents from the Close.

Martin and Miranda had parked about five centimetres – well, maybe twenty – over the boundary. Grumfuttocks went storming into the kitchen, his poor little dog in tow, and started screeching

'You have absolutely no consideration. I could have been killed. I had to get out into the road on the way back from my walk with the dog and a car could easily have run me over,' *oh what a joyful thought, crossed Val's mind before she could stop it* – 'and you didn't even warn me about all this disruption. Who do you think you are?'

'Graham,' said Val, 'we sent you an invitation. You m – '. But she got no further.

'An invitation you knew I wouldn't accept. This behaviour is becom – ' It was Dr Di who saved the day. 'Don't I remember you from the hospital?' she asked, all charm and joy. 'One of the invaluable portering team? How are you enjoying retirement?' Grumfuttocks looked like he was going to explode all over the canapes, turned on his heels and they never had any dealings with him again. Sad but true.

The rest of the afternoon went off without a hitch and Val felt a bit more like she belonged there. It had been worth it after all.

***

'What made you decide?' asked Lawrence.

'The run in with Grumfuttocks sealed it for me. But it was Mrs Khan who started me thinking,' said Valerie. *Why am I not surprised? Lawrence asked himself.* 'She made me take a step back to distance myself from the heavy lifting.'

'And where did that take you?'

'I realised that now I'm married, I'm a proper adult. Not that I wasn't before, of course, I had a responsible job and everything. But that house was where I grew up and it was left to me by my parents. I've never really left home. It's time to move on and reinvent myself as a wife.'

'Not just a wife, my love. You are so much more.'

Let me share something with you – this is one marriage I really want to work.

***

Back at Mrs Khan's, Lally and Mrs Khan were hosting a tea tasting for a few neighbours from her own road. Chelsea had appointed herself Snack Distributor in Chief and was doing a grand job.

'Are you going to market this?' they were asked.

'Probably not. It's a bit of fun, really, something to keep us occupied and use a bit of the creative side of our brains.' In spite of the answer she'd just given, Lally was pleased that it was considered to be good enough to sell.

'Well, I'd buy some from you, if you make enough to want to sell it.'

Mrs K and Lally gave each other what might be construed as a meaningful look and asked Chelsea to take round another plate of homemade snacks.

'Could this be another string to my bow?' thought Lally, who was even more interested in finding ways of supplementing her income now that Del appeared to be off the scene for good. 'I'll hold you to that,' she said. 'In fact, when we get the first commercial packets through, I'll give you the chance to buy them before anyone else.'

Mrs Khan wondered how Mrs Ford was getting on. She might phone later to enquire. Better still, wait for her to phone, just in case the stress had proved too much.

In the event, when Val called that evening, they both had plenty to report and decided to meet up for coffee in the promenade café the following morning.

At least the New Year had started well for someone.

THE SERPENT AND THE SPHINX
Middle Eastern Dance

'Is this really me?' Dorothy was totally staggered at what she was doing or more to the point, feeling.

The women hadn't bargained for this, not being inveigled to take part in a lesson, no matter how basic the moves.

'Woooo!' Lally was proving to be an expert.

'Okay, ladies, now Camel Walk!' Louisa was an inspirational teacher.

Helena was throwing herself into it like it'd been her life's sole purpose and other members felt quite stiff by comparison.

The talk had been fascinating – about how it was originally by women for women and still was in many places; and how it'd changed with colonisation when costuming had altered drastically and it had been turned into a cabaret form.

The moves they'd been asked to do were simple: circles, figures of eight, hip drops and the like but not all the women felt that comfortable. Maybe if they'd known in advance but having it sprung on them like that! It was a bit much, really, but come to think of it, most of them wouldn't have turned up if they'd known. They were trying to give it their best shot, do it justice; and the speaker, Louisa Cherry, seemed pleased with their efforts. 'We all feel a bit strange at first because of where the movement's concentrated and it's so different from our Western dance, where the centre of gravity is high, but once that music starts, it'll come to you so easily, you'll wonder why you never did it before.'

And she'd been right. There was something about the earthy elegance of the rhythms and the haunting sounds of the instruments that simply made you want to move. Not all the women were that relaxed about it, though. Over the break, comments like 'it's not really right, is it, drawing attention to yourself like that' and 'it made me feel a bit like I should be auditioning for a place in a bordello' could be heard but by and large, the members had had a lovely time. After all, Louisa had been entertaining and so knowledgeable. She'd been to the Middle East to learn and even spoke a bit of Arabic.

'Do you teach in the area?' asked Lally.

'No, I live in Bristol and it's a bit of a trek on a regular basis. Leave me your details and I'll see if I can find someone for you.'

How Lally would ever fit it in was a total mystery but she felt this was what she needed. It made her feel womanly again and she so wanted that. There was still no word from Del and apart from walks and occasional chats with Gos and the odd word with Lawrence – he really wasn't as bad as the rumours had suggested – her social contact was all with women. 'Nothing wrong with that,' she thought, but she missed the things that come with having a male companion.

'If you find somewhere to learn,' said Dorothy to her, 'could you let me know?' Now that was a bolt from the blue, if anything ever was.

In the safety of the kitchen, Mrs Khan was sorting out the refreshments. She'd brought another of the teas they'd created to try out on the assembled company. She was deep in thought and uncharacteristically not really living in the moment, her usual dwelling place.

'Mrs Ford,' she said, 'I have an idea. Could you come to see me briefly when you have time?'

'No sooner the word than the deed. I'll pop in when I've finished up here.'

Lally and Helena were going through the cupboards to see if there was anything suitable to turn into costumes.

'I tell you what,' said Lally. 'Why don't we go for a recce round the charity shops, see if we can find anything there?'

'You're on.' So the two women said thank you to Louise and took their leave.

**

The Wizard was getting restless. He'd heard nothing from the estate agent and wanted to be sure he'd get in first.

'Sorry, but we've still heard nothing from the vendor.'

Glory be, he thought, do these Brits not want to take their lives forward?

**

'Mrs Evans – (Lally to you and me) – has been a little worried about staying in her house. She can't sell it without permission from her absent husband and is a trifle concerned that it is now a bit small. Chelsea is not small baby anymore. She is finding things she needs for her new profession and other endeavours very space consuming. Do you think you might like to rent April Cottage to her? Maybe for reduced rent – *or no rent at all, she thought but didn't make so bold as to say* – in return for acting as caretaker and curator? If it works out, possibly when Mr Evans makes himself known, she – or they, if he returns for good – could purchase it from you. '

'Leave it with me, Mrs Khan,' she said. 'We'll mull it over and see whether or not it would work.'

'Not perfect solution,' thought Mrs Khan, 'but imperfect solution better than no solution at all.'

I'll second that.

GK BLUES

Was it a January thing? Gos wondered. You start on January First thinking there was a new start in the offing and then by Jan second, things are worse than they've ever been. Real or perceived? He speculated. Ren had gone off for a so-called spa fortnight with a 'few friends' (more likely to be one particular friend, he thought cynically), the weather was appalling, he had writer's block and all in all, he'd really not found the return to the Khan (West Virginia) Residence had been all he'd hoped for. Or, indeed, a single thing that he'd hoped for.

The festive season had been anything but. Gos Jnr had elected to go to his girlfriend in California, Cher had spent the whole time on her phone, Ren was busy organising her holiday and as things were turning out, he'd spent a lot of time wondering why he'd bothered to waste his money on the air fare. Next year Cher would be away at med school – *why were all the women in the family doctors? (Except Ren) flitted through his mind, apropos of nothing* – and it'd just be the two of them. OMG.

Looking out over the acres of land that came with the building usually known as the family home and gazing at the swimming pool that an Olympian would have considered too big, he seriously started to question whether or not he really believed he'd be able to talk Ren into swopping this for a terraced three-bedroomed house with a courtyard garden in Bristol. More to the point, did he want to anymore? He was missing the gentle pace in Stackton, the sound of the waves breaking on the sand, the easy-going people with their unassuming manners. And, he was missing that lovely young woman and her sweet daughter. Oh no – was he allowed to even think that in the twenty first century? There'd be bound to someone out there who'd misunderstand and suspect him of all manner of unspeakable desires.

'Why is it,' he asked himself, 'that there are such different standards for men and women?' This had become a regular line of self-questioning. All those years, Ren had taken lover after lover (and he suspected that 'taken' was exactly the right word) and he just had to go along with it, if it weren't going to mean breaking up the family with all that that entails, but he'd had one short-lived fling with a colleague and the entire claque had turned on him like a school of sharks in a herring fishery.

The first time, it'd cut him like a knife but he'd forgiven her. There was too much as stake not to. But there'd been a long succession after that and each one severed another tie.

Dad would say 'Follow heart. Always more reliable than head.' Good advice. His head was sending him round in circles. Trouble was, his heart wasn't serving him any better.

Mum would tell him to have a cup of tea and another piece of cake. No chance of that. Ren wouldn't allow a piece of cake in the house, not even on Christmas Day.

You know what? Ren wasn't there. He could eat a whole litre tub of ice cream unaided if he wanted and there'd be no-one there to make snide comments, pull faces or inform him of the dangers of sugar and fat. He got the car keys and headed for the Mall.

***

Back in Stackton, the Wizard was impatient. The realtor wouldn't tell him which house it was, so he took himself down to Barretts Avenue and tried to ascertain which one was empty and waiting for a new owner. As it wasn't by any means clear – too many holiday homes – he stopped a friendly-looking stranger in the street and asked if she knew which one was up for sale.

'Thing is, ma'am, I forgot my cell phone and can't remember which number the estate agent told me to meet her.'

'Ah, it must be Val's place. April Cottage. Just along there.'

'Thank you ma'am. Have a nice day.'

He found it easily enough. 'Nice forecourt,' he thought. 'That'll easily hold two of those dinky cars that the Brits drive around in.' He went and peered through the window. 'That wall can come down and the whole of the bottom floor can be turned into an office. This is looking good.'

Now all that was needed was the go-ahead from the vendor. He'd go to the showroom and give the realtor a proper talking-to.

***

It was with more than a little surprise that Gos looked up from his breakfast – toast (a mountain of it covered in butter that would cause Ren to faint even at the idea) and a pot of coffee that had been refreshed at least three times – to see Michelle standing in the doorway.

'Why Garss,' she drawled, 'Ah hadn't expected to see you here.'

'The feeling's mutual,' he said. 'Did you come back from the spa early?' Michelle tried hard to conceal the fact that she had no idea what he was talking about but wasn't a great actress. 'Why, yes. Yes, ah did.' 'And Ren didn't tell you I'd be here?' 'Hell, no. Ah guess –' 'Cut the crap, Michelle. She told me she was going away with friends to a spa. You're not telling me that you weren't included, or at least invited. Or are you?' Michelle knew the game was up, at least for her. 'Well, thing is, yes ah was, but ah didn't want to go. And then it all went quiet and ah just sort of thought it wasn't gonna happen. Bill and ah went away for the festivities – stayed with Lucianna and her new beau – and got back yesterday. Thought ah'd check in to see how Renate was getting along. She didn't tell me you'd be staying beyond the twenty fifth. Ah thought she'd be here alone.' 'I'm sorry to disappoint you. I guess she's off with whoever her latest squeeze is. He must be pretty special if she's not even felt she can share the details with you.' Michelle looked extremely uncomfortable and Gos felt as if he'd overstepped the mark. He liked Michelle. She was a decent sort of woman with an open nature and a kind heart. In spite of her forthright, uncensored conversation, delivered in that gorgeous accent, languid and sensuous. There wasn't an ounce of malice in her. Far from it. Gos had often thought she erred on the side of being too kind. Putting her on the spot like this wasn't fair. 'I don't expect you to betray any confidences. We both know what she's like.' 'Thing is, Garss, you're a truly lovely man, honest you are,' she looked embarrassed but went on 'but you're no go-getter, are you? Renate's a gorgeous woman – *so I would hope, thought Gos, the amount of money that goes into resculpting her face and body* – and she needs someone a bit more dynamic than a college professor.' 'Right. I appreciate your honesty. I wish Ren would honour me with the same courtesy.' Gos was a little winded but not totally surprised.

He regained his composure and closed the laptop. No chance of being able to work today.

'Would you like to have sex with me, Garss?'

'No thanks,' he said, remembering his manners. He wondered fleetingly if his mother would be proud of him being able to remain polite under stress.

Michelle stopped in the doorway and turned back to him 'You know, Garss,' she said, 'Renate is one of mah oldest friends. We've been like sisters since Cher was born and ah love her dearly. But you deserve better.'

His mother had always told him that compromise is a Bad Thing. 'Just means that two people end up dissatisfied.' Looked like she'd been right. He'd spent his entire married life compromising – or rather giving in to Ren's demands – and sure as hell, they were both looking for satisfaction elsewhere, Ren with other men and Gos with a change of job and country. Better to know now than later, while there was still time for them both to salvage something of their lives.

He opened the laptop again and booked a ticket back to England.

FEBRUARY

GARDEN GNOMES: THEIR HISTORY, CULTURE AND ECOLOGICAL SIGNIFICANCE

'Mrs Khan.'

'Mr Speaker, I would like to ask if my garden will suffer because injured gnome gifted me by my sons is lying in my shed with broken arm which has not been attended to?'

'Very fair question, Mrs Khan. I would advise that you err on the side of caution and get his arm repaired as soon as possible.' Gerald was delighted that the women were joining in the fun so whole-heartedly. 'It's worth bearing in mind that the ill-fortune visited on us when we neglect our Gnomish friends and protectors isn't necessarily just restricted to the garden. There are excellent gnome surgeons to be found if you are unable to undertake the surgery yourself.'

'Thank you.' Said Val. 'Jenny: you wanted to ask Gerald a question.'

'You spoke very eloquently about the paucity of female gnomes. Could you explain how the species reproduces itself?'

'You may have heard of a phenomenon known as parthenogenesis, where females reproduce without the intervention of males. This is not the case for gnomes, however. Reproduction occurs by spontaneous generation. Some people think that these creatures are manufactured. Nothing could be further from the truth. The details of the process are cryptic and whilst I have been honoured with the opportunity to observe it, which, I'm sure you will agree is beyond being privileged, I am unable to share the details with you, for fear of incurring their wrath.'

'Time for one more question. Yes, Moira, what would you like to know?'

'How do the gnomes distinguish between the good fairies like the pixies and the bad ones like the goblins?'

'Luckily, there is no need. The fairies with evil intent only need to see the gnome to be dissuaded from entering the garden.'

'Thank you Gerald. Now, I think we should continue our discussion over refreshments in the dining room. Shall we thank Gerald again for his very erudite talk which we've all enjoyed greatly on this wet, grey February afternoon?'

Valerie started the applause and the W.I. joined in enthusiastically. Sometimes, it does us a great deal of good not to take life too seriously.

***

In the kitchen. Lally had been preparing the drinks using another of her own blends. She and Mrs Khan were having a great deal of fun trying out different mixtures and the members of the W.I. were only too happy to be employed, albeit not gainfully, as tea-tasters. So far, they'd only had one complete disaster but all the others had met with approval. There were two clear leaders though, and they were thinking very seriously about packaging them and selling them at the Summer Fair. Lally was also having thoughts of adding *The Development of the Ultimate W.I. Blend of Tea* to this year's Bucket List, but maybe it would be best to wait until the new season.

She was very unsure regarding Val's kind offer to let the two of them live in her house in return for her taking over the bills and keeping it in good condition. It would help her a great deal, Val had explained, because it was never good for a house to be left empty, particularly in a seaside town and she'd heard of places being invaded by squatters. This last wasn't entirely true, but Val was pretty sure someone had said it about somewhere or other and it might swing things in her favour. To Val, it was the perfect solution.

Lally's concerns were related to the long term. She knew that people thought she was over-cautious in all things, but wasn't that inevitable if there was a small child in the equation? At some point, Val would want the house back and what would she do then? Little Chelsea had had a massive upheaval in her life already and she wasn't even four yet. Best to avoid more disruptions if they weren't absolutely inescapable. She thought she'd discuss it with Mrs Khan and see if she had any words of wisdom on the subject.

But for the moment, she was enjoying hearing the comments on the tea, ranging from 'this is the best one yet' through to 'yuck! Too strong! It'd dissolve the cups!' It just proves you can't please everyone.

***

On the way home, Mrs Khan was viewing the garden statuary with a completely new eye. No longer were these just bits of frippery designed to bring a smile to the face of some, whilst offending others by their kitsch and increasingly vulgar manifestations, but guardians of the microworlds in which they had been placed and evidently ruled. She did wonder, though, what the point was in a fishing gnome when there was no water within striking distance of the rod; or what was seemingly an advertisement for smoking a pipe when we all know that it's bad for our health. Maybe it was different for gnomes. 'No discernible lungs, I guess,' passed through her brain as she noticed a broadly smiling member of the community sitting on his mushroom – fly agaric, naturally – puffing away.

'Maybe we should see if we can get our gnomes together for partying,' she pondered. 'Easter celebration, maybe, or May Day. They deserve time off, also, with such a responsible job.'

As she walked through her front door, she thought it might be sensible to keep such thoughts to herself if she was going to maintain the illusion of being a sane and entirely rational woman.

***

The Wizard was feeling snubbed because his very generous offer on April Cottage had still not been accepted. 'Tell the vendor he has twenty four hours or I withdraw.' This message had been duly passed on and had elicited no response. Clearly another line of action was necessary, but he couldn't think what on earth it might be. He'd made a mistake by issuing an ultimatum as it had shown the vendor how keen he was and given them the upper hand. Was he losing his negotiating skills? Something about this little town had got to him. He wanted to be here and to make his mark on it. Time for some serious rethinking.

With that uppermost in his mind, he packed his case and got ready to leave in the morning. He'd only be gone a few weeks. Maybe things would have moved on by the time he returned.

***

In the Reynolds household, Dorothy was regretting her decision to give Gloria a chance at chocolate making. So far, different batches of chocolate had coagulated, burned or separated. The trouble was, her mind was really not on the job in hand and more to the point, her heart not in it. Dorothy wanted to cry but was too well brought up to do that in public.

'Gloria,' she said. 'I'm sorry, really I am, but this is not going to work. Apart from the risk of bankruptcy, what with the damage to the tools and the ruining of the raw materials, making chocolates is something I'm passionate about. Some of us just aren't cut out for it.'

Gloria could see that Dorothy was right so made her apologies and left. Back to the starting blocks or, more specifically, to Mrs Khan's to see if they could work out the next step.

DONKEY DAYS

Mrs Khan and Chelsea were happily feeding the donkeys with the packed lunch they'd brought with them to the Sanctuary. At least, Chelsea was. Mrs Khan hadn't realised her sandwich box was empty until she felt the need for a cheese and pickle roll. 'Hope you enjoyed it, boy,' she said. He didn't bother to reply.

Buoyed up by the successes – both achieved and ongoing – of the W.I. women, Jenny decided it was time to take the plunge herself. Not literally, of course, her Bucket List entry had nothing to do with either swimming or diving.

It was with this is mind that the three of them made their way to the Donkey Sanctuary about ten miles along the road from Stackton, a beautiful place in sprawling grounds, partially tree covered and whilst not within sight of the sea itself, the journey there ran for the whole of its length along the coast road. 'Lovely day for it,' said Mrs Khan, piling into the car with her young buddy, who was ecstatic at spending the day out in the open with the donkeys and "Arty K". Jenny was driving and had already explained why this had been her Bucket List entry.

'I was kicked once by a horse,' she told Mrs Khan. 'It wasn't the horse's fault. Some idiot decided to tease her as I was walking past. She reared up and kicked me in the back. I've been scared of them ever since but donkeys are more docile and I think if I can get to be comfortable with them, it'll help me with horses.'

'Any particular reason you want to feel okay with horses?' asked Mrs K.

'I come from a horsey family and miss out on an awful lot because I'm too scared to join in.'

'Ever been to Gnome Sanctuary, Mrs Bennett?' Mrs Khan wasn't quite sure herself why she made the enquiry but never mind, it was done now.

'Never. Have you?' Jenny looked mystified.

'We went as family when my boys were young. Never since.' Mrs Khan resolved to ask Gos if he'd like a return visit with Lally and Chelsea.

'Well, let's see how today goes. If I survive it, maybe a close up and personal look at some of Britain's little folk would be the next thing for the agenda.' Jenny couldn't honestly imagine why on earth anyone would devote an area of precious ground to the protection of clay models, and ugly ones at that; and considered that anyone setting such a project in motion must be slightly nuts. Furthermore, anyone paying good money for entry to keep the business running must have more money than sense. Lots more. All the same, the talk the previous week had been entertaining and illuminating, so she was a little more kindly disposed than she would have been without it.

Mrs Khan was quite surprised to discover that Chelsea wasn't really that interested in the shop, getting far more fun and satisfaction from interaction with the donkeys. Of course, she enjoyed the ice cream enormously and would have continued to indulge herself far more than Lally would like given the chance, but really, what she wanted was to be out there with them, chatting and stroking their furry bodies.

'Ears, Arty K. Big ears,' she announced, pointing at a particularly raggedy looking beast. 'Want to stroke them!'

she said. Mrs Khan lifted her up and held her close to the fence. Far from the clumsy attempt she'd expected from so young a child, Chelsea was gentle and sensitive. The donkey, an elderly gentleman called Frogman – who knows why? – looked like he was getting as much from the interaction as young Chelsea herself. 'Nice dockey,' said Chelsea, 'good dockey.' Her face was set in a look of loving wonder and it betrayed no sign of tiring of communing with her new chum. 'Shall we see if we can adopt him?' asked Mrs Khan. 'Peeze, Arty K.' She put the little girl back down on the ground and the two of them walked hand in hand to the Adoption Shed. It was impossible to know which of them was getting more from the day. Mrs Khan's grandchildren had been born and grown up in the USA and she'd missed all this. Maybe Lally would be agreeable to her being an Honorary Granny. She'd ask when she got the chance.

Jenny, meanwhile, had overcome her apprehension in the presence of Medium-sized Equines – as the keeper kept describing them – and was well on the way to signing up as a volunteer. She'd been visiting for some time, just getting used to being near the animals but hadn't had the courage to stroke them and definitely not to walk with them.

The keeper was impressed with the rapport built up in such a short time and was giving her the lowdown on what it took to keep the enterprise going. If she wanted to work directly with the animals, she'd have to do a day's training in Donkey Care, coming complete with a Certificate of Proficiency. It wouldn't be cheap, but so enraptured was she now that she'd conquered her fear, she didn't mind the expense. At the back of her mind and unspoken had been the hope that this would be the outcome. She was only working part-time and could easily give a day a week to the Sanctuary.

'What sort of things would I be able to do?' she asked.

'Anything at all that we have on offer across all departments. Maybe you'd like to work in the shop before getting directly involved with donkey care. It'd give you greater insight into how we do things here.' It wasn't quite what she'd had in mind but she was up for anything.

Jenny was walking Tessie round the courtyard when Mrs Khan and Chelsea came into view. Chelsea, now a veteran with her own brand of donkey care, ran up to her and gently stroked Tessie's side.

'We're coming to adopt Frogman,' offered Mrs Khan.

'Good,' thought Jenny, 'a bit more revenue for the Sanctuary.' How quickly we sink into the culture of our chosen environment.

The adoption process wasn't as straightforward as Mrs Khan had hoped. Frogman, it transpired, was a very elderly donkey indeed and probably wouldn't be with us for more than a few months. Rather than Chelsea having to face the loss of her new buddy, surely it would be best to choose a different animal.

'Want Fogman,' said Chelsea.

'All these other donkeys need someone to love them too.' Mrs Khan pointed at the board offering more than twenty potential wards.

'Want Fogman,' said Chelsea again.

'How about the three of us go round the fields and meet the other donkeys. You can decide which one you'd like to have as your friend,' said Jenny.

'Fogman,' repeated Chelsea, this time with a light stamp.

In the event, the three of them wandered around the paddocks together – returning to Frogman so he wouldn't feel abandoned – while Jenny explained that although it wouldn't be his name on Chelsea's certificate, she could still have a photo of him; and the other donkeys would be so proud of her for choosing an animal in greater need, they'd all give him extra help and love. Reluctantly, Chelsea chose a different one; but when Jenny brought her over to be stroked and befriended, she was such a sweet, affectionate creature that any lingering objections were forgotten. Jenny took her to join the keeper, so that the three of them could walk Nancy round the grounds together, while Mrs Khan rested on one of the benches.

'Nice Nancy,' crooned Chelsea, 'pitty Nancy,' clearly in love.

They collected her Welcome Pack and had a last drink in the café. Before leaving, they bought some carrots and gave both Nancy and Frogman a final meal.

Jenny was clearly thrilled to have achieved all she had and got down to teaching them both everything she'd learned during her day as a paying keeper – quite an extensive bank of knowledge. 'Not really my thing,' thought Mrs Khan, 'but important to allow Mrs Bennett her moment in the sun.' Chelsea was poring over the bits she'd been given in her Adoption Pack, singing to herself contentedly; and Mrs Khan was wondering how best to broach the subject of becoming a surrogate granny for Chelsea.

As it turned out, it wasn't necessary. Chelsea asked Lally herself if Mrs K could be her granny, so it was agreed with no need for discussion.

'So much good fortune,' observed Mrs Khan on her way back. 'Perhaps Mr Gnome had a better life in our home than I gave credit for.' As she was unlocking the door, Tigger rubbed his furry flanks against her legs, purring loudly. Stepping across the threshold into the hallway, 'Had a good day, Mum?' came floating across to her from the lounge. 'Indeed,' she called back. 'Indeed,' she thought, 'so many good days now, such occurrences are commonplace and they're not really worthy of special mention.'

Have the Stackton-on-Sea W.I. discovered the meaning of life?

LOOSE ENDS AND BROKEN GNOMES

The short, February days came and went. It wasn't a particularly bad month. There was no snow or ice, no untimely heatwave; nobody reported an invasion of green men (or women) from Mars and there were no sightings of rare beasts that could threaten anything dire to the countryside or its inhabitants. In short, it wasn't much to write home about.

Mrs Khan was always a little irritated with herself at this time of year, as she longed for the dawning of the day when she could get out in the garden again and get going with all the things that needed doing. 'Can't afford to waste days at my time of life and certainly not wish them away. Too few of them left,' she said to Gos, who had finally settled down in earnest once more to write his book. He was quite happy with the lack of stimulation, because it meant the only thing that distracted him was the sudden need for copious cups of coffee and pieces of cake.

***

Dorothy was amassing files on possible countries for the Cocoa Bean Adventure, as it had become known, so she was content enough whilst moving no further forward with her plans. Val and Lawrence, having enjoyed the short cruise at the end of last year, had found a last minute offer for two weeks touring the Caribbean and that's what they were doing with their friends Miranda and Martin. They'd be back in time for the March W.I. meeting and some of the women had put their names on the rota for looking after the cats and dogs. Bodkin and Winston didn't appear to care much, as long as their bowls were filled. That's what they'd all expected, of course, the moreso since the October meeting, but Hector and Billy were another matter. They'd been found temporary homes for most of the holiday but there were three days when they had to stop at Bayfield, being walked three times a day by kind dog lovers. They'd never been in kennels and Val felt they were are bit old and set in their ways to start now. She'd considered asking Grumfuttocks if he'd like to help out, in the interests of good neighbourliness, but knew it was just a bit of mischief on her part, so quelled the urge. The two dogs were ecstatic the minute they heard footsteps coming along the path and rewarded their companions with good behaviour and a lot of love. They looked so forlorn when it was time to go home, it was difficult for their new guardians not to take them back with them, but with dogs of their own, they couldn't really accommodate any extras.

***

For Lally, things hadn't changed materially at all and as for Helena, well, she was busy with her college course and loading herself up with more and more writing and creating a bucket list of her own.

Many of the women worked part-time or volunteered in different capacities, whilst others were like Gina and ran their businesses from their back bedrooms, organising work to fit round other commitments and the WI.

Gina's husband, Gil, was out all day and all three of their children had moved out to go to university or otherwise make lives of their own, so Gina was able to determine her own fate to a very large extent. This month, a lot of her time was spent with choral scores and YouTube, learning the parts for the pieces they were singing in the choir. She was loving it, was grateful to both Val and Lawrence for egging her on to do it. She was absolutely determined to make it work for her.

***

'Thank goodness only twenty eight days in this month,' commented Mrs Khan over their supper that evening. 'First of March means springtime and, my boy, *(with a twinkle in her eye)* that's when young man's fancy turns to love.'

'Don't get your hopes up, mum. There's so much to sort out and I'm still hoping Ren and I can work something out so we can stay together.' What he said was absolutely true but deep inside, he felt pretty sure that there was no real chance of that happening. Neither he nor Ren were that interested in maintaining the status quo and what would be the point? At least the kids, at the age they were, would be unaffected.

Mrs Khan was still unable to comprehend what it must be like to see your marriage falling apart, even though she observed it in others many times and had done her best to truly empathise. Her own had been as blissful as any marriage could ever aspire to be. Of course, they'd had their difficult times but it had been rock solid and there'd never been the slightest hint that it wouldn't be possible to work through the blips. When Mr Khan died suddenly from an asymptomatic brain tumour, never having had so much as a headache or needed a paracetamol for toothache, her world had fallen apart but she was profoundly relieved that he hadn't suffered. Her lasting regret was that she'd been unable to say goodbye and wish him bon voyage.

Suddenly finding that she had time on her hands, she discovered the poster for the Stackton-on-Sea W.I. at the local library and had never looked back.

Pootling around in the shed, she found Mr Gnome and his severed right arm. 'Ah, let's ask Gos if he can find time to restore you to your former glory,' she said to him, remembering that gnomes like to be spoken to. And then, with her tongue firmly lodged in her cheek: 'After all, we know now that you've been looking after us. Or maybe not'. She was happy to play along with the mythology to a certain extent, especially with Chelsea, who loved the stories the women were relating to her from the talk, but 'maybe keep own head properly fixed to shoulders.'

An excellent idea and one that many of us could learn from.

MARCH

THE ART OF THE PERFUMIER

Dorothy was in seventh heaven. This, surely, was what they meant by being in the moment, mindfulness, Zen – all those things so much in vogue. Her Chocolate Laboratory was immaculate, everything beautifully laid out, clean, in exactly the right order for creating delicious, life enhancing edibles. Today was not for a fair, commissions, anything at all beyond the sheer, sensual pleasure involved in the art of making.

It pained her to admit it, but even if Gloria had proved to be an excellent chocolatier, she would not have liked sharing this sacred sanctum with anyone else. She would have to find another way round the dilemma of finding herself spread a little too thin at times. She hoped Gloria had not been too disappointed.

Dorothy loved the meetings. She truly, truly did. But why had no-one ever asked her to talk about *The Art of the Chocolatier*? It was just as interesting and just as skilled. AND you could eat the product. She didn't want to be pushy but frankly, she really considered they should to want to know about her career. It was as important as anything any of them had done. 'Well, maybe not Dr Di, she conceded. 'She's been a GP for practically all her life and has no doubt saved a few lives in her time.' But all the others, well, she was sure she'd made as big a contribution to well-being as the rest of them.

It'd been an accident. Being born the only child to

elderly parents who adored her but had grown up at a time when it was believed there was no point in educating girls, they'd not thought it worth her while staying on at school, so being a pharmacist was completely out of the question. O'levels were okay but beyond that, well, what was the point? She'd only marry and have children and all that schooling would have gone for nothing. It wasn't even as if she'd wanted to be a nurse – perfectly acceptable as a vocation for a daughter who would herself end up rearing the next generation; and one they would have been enthusiastic about – but no, she wanted to do *science*. What on earth for?

While tempering the chocolate, absorbing the smell and the soft, luxuriant texture of the molten gloop (*my word, not hers*), she wondered again how on earth the early experiments with those big, unwieldy beans had ever resulted in the vast variety of products now commonplace all over the world. Notoriously difficult to grow, yet servicing a colossal industry offering comfort, sustenance, even medicine at one time in the form of tea for travellers suffering from altitude sickness; and surely everyone knew that a little bit was good for the heart. Of course, there were those who claimed it to have aphrodisiac properties, but it seemed to Dorothy that that had been claimed for practically every tasty – and not so tasty – foodstuff known to humanity. She glossed over its contribution to the cocaine industry, but was happy to acknowledge that in spite of the long history of chocolate production, it was such a complex substance that an awful lot about it was simply undiscovered. 'Is it too late to contribute to the knowledge base?' she wondered. Only time would tell.

Stumbling accidentally into the chocolate industry had saved Dorothy's life, or so she believed. Still reeling from the break up – by her parents – of the only relationship that ever meant anything to her and wondering what on earth she was going to do with her life now she couldn't get the professional training she longed for, she got herself a job in a chocolate factory to tide her over and earn some cash until she found something she might devote her life to. She knew there was no destiny for her as wife and mother. During the first few days in what she originally thought was a temporary place of work, her fate was sealed. From then on, she'd wanted nothing but to spend her time learning all she could and trying out her own ideas. After six years in the factory, she found work in a small, independent company making individual chocolates by hand. She loved this even more. She'd been a small daisy in a ginormous garden before, and there'd been a special department where people came up with ideas and developed them. Everything had to be tested to the nth degree, approved by quality control panels, tried out on the public – the list goes on. But here, it was a matter of them all mucking in together, and everyone could offer their ideas and they'd be given a fair trial, even if they sounded whacky. Testing consisted of putting some free samples out on the counter and asking customers what they thought. Proving herself to be an excellent student and practitioner of the art, she was given more and more responsibility until by the time the owners retired, it was effectively her project, so they gave her the chance to buy the business. 'In real terms, it's yours already,' said the Manager (also masquerading as the owner, Chief Chocolatier, Development Manager and Chief Taster, as well as any number of admin officers). Thus, after a visit to the bank, she became the proud owner of Reynolds, Handmade Chocolate for the Connoisseur. On her own retirement (when she was fifty five) fiercely protective of all the wonderful recipes she'd created, she'd moved to Stackton from Bristol and transported all her equipment into a purpose built shed and turned it into a private haven for the manufacture of sweetmeats for the discerning.

She rarely thought about Linda anymore. She honestly didn't blame her parents. In those days, same sex relationships were a scandal that could ruin someone's life, and they hadn't wanted that to happen to her. No-one wants to see the life of their child destroyed by an unfortunate liaison and in any case, they'd believed it to be a fad. She'd like to know what had happened to her dear friend though; if the woman she once thought she'd spend her life with had been happy and made a good go of it all. Every attempt to track her down online and through other channels, like meeting points in magazines and contacting her old school had proved unfruitful and she wondered if her family had sent her down the route her own parents had tried for her: to find a suitable man and marry her to him. Whatever had transpired, she hoped Linda was happy.

She knew she'd need to start looking in earnest for a plantation if she was going to make it this year. It'd been so busy, with all the extra events the W.I. had staged to raise money for the *Let's Share Allotment*, and normal life had to continue whatever the W.I. were doing. She'd wondered about taking on an apprentice. From what she'd heard, you got paid for doing that and the person employed came out with a skill to make a career from. She'd give it some serious thought after she'd done her field visit.

With several kilos of handmade chocolates cooling overnight, Dorothy sat out in the garden with a mug of delicious hot cocoa and wondered how they'd taken the step from the drink that had been the original produce from the cacao beans to the stuff that you could cut up and eat. It must say somewhere and she'd look it up if she remembered.

How could anyone not share her love of both the process and the product? Still, even if they didn't want her to talk to them about it at the WI, they were very happy to accept her donations and had suggested many times that they pay her for them. They were appreciative of all her trials, giving her feedback and encouragement and that kept her fulfilled.

It'd all worked out okay in the end and to her way of thinking, that's probably the best that any of us can hope for.

**

Gloria hadn't been heartbroken in the slightest. She'd found the workroom too hot, the pervading aroma of sweet, sticky chocolate too cloying and for the life of her, couldn't see the attraction. After all, you could go and buy yourself a big block of the stuff for under a pound without all the bother. Still, she was worried.

'Mrs Khan,' she said, 'I don't know if it's just the chocolate making that I don't get on with or if I'm so eaten up about Jamie that nothing is ever going to work.' 'This is progress,' thought Mrs Khan, replying 'It was good for both you and Miss Reynolds to have this experience. Lessons must have been learned by both.'

'Yes, I know that, but I'm not sure how useful the lessons are. I mean, discovering I'm not one of the world's natural chocolatiers doesn't really get me very far forward, does it?'

'Yes and no. You have discovered that there could be greater problems than not wishing to create sweets and that your relationship with your delightful son could be one of them. By the way, you haven't mentioned Jamie recently. How are they getting on?'

'It all seems to be fine. She's seven months now, nearly eight, so quite a long way through. I've been trying to keep out of their way because I heard on the grapevine that they were thinking of moving to get away from "my interfering"' Gloria paused, tears in her eyes, looking down at the floor of Mrs Khan's lounge with a great deal of concentration. 'They didn't say it to me, of course, and it could have been presented to me as a done deal, so at least I have the chance to try to change.' She could speak no further, so took another sip of tea and a half-hearted bite of cake. Her mind wandering again, Mrs Khan wondered how it was that they all stayed slim, given the range and volume of cakes they consumed. Coming back to the point, she asked 'But they are not going to make that move, you think?'

'No. At least, I don't think so. I mean, would you have wanted to move when you were seven months pregnant?' No, I wouldn't, thought Mrs Khan, but I had no mother-in-law trying to run my life. No mother either, for that matter. Still, she felt very sorry for Gloria and over the months, she'd come to understand more and more why Gloria was finding it all so hard. What she said was 'There was no need for me to do so. My life was very different from that of young people these days. Are you sure proposed move was nothing more than desire for bigger accommodation? Stackton-on-Sea is not that cheap and for what they could get for their house here, they could buy more rooms and a bigger garden elsewhere.'

'They've got a four bedroomed house up behind the marsh. Her father bought it for them as a wedding present.' Ah, thought Mrs Khan, another source of anguish. Gloria had always struggled just to put food in Jamie's mouth, let alone provide luxuries, but in spite of it all, she'd done an excellent job.

'I think, Mrs Fisher,' said Mrs Khan, 'what you should do is try out many things. Not think the first thing you attempt has to work out or it's all failure. Maybe accompany some of the women on their Bucket List quests. Their ambitions won't be yours but will give you extra experience and insights into other pursuits.'

Gloria finished her tea and gathered up her things. 'Thanks, Mrs Khan,' she said. 'I'll see what I can do.'

THE ASSESSMENT OF PERSONALITY THROUGH THE STUDY OF MUGS

Lally was unpacking the remaining bits she'd brought with her. There really wasn't very much, as Val had left her entire household in situ and besides, if Del ever turned up back at the house, he'd need everything himself. She was a bit concerned about maintaining the aquarium, but as she'd been assured that Val was trying to find a way of getting it transported to Bayfield, she was just hoping it would be sooner rather than later, or at least before she'd caused everything in it to die. Chelsea was 'helping', of course.

'I wonder if Freud ever studied mugs,' she thought, remembering her A' Level Psychology lectures while going through the first of the boxes. 'Probably not. He was interested in more spicy topics than how we drink our tea. Come to think of it, did they even use mugs in those days?'

Chelsea disappeared upstairs to unpack her toy box. She seemed happy enough and the pre-school people hadn't suggested there were any difficulties with her behaviour or anything, so Lally thought they'd both got off lightly with the upheavals of the last few months. At least, she hoped so. It was good to see Gos around again, though. She liked him.

'This tea blending is great fun but it leaves appalling stains on the crockery,' she said out loud, casting around for the stuff she cleaned Granma Edie's dentures with.

'That'll do the trick.'

Arranging the mugs tidily in the cupboard next to the sink, she started to look more closely at the emblems printed on the china. Do they say anything about you? That, she decided, would have been a far more interesting project for her psychology course: *The Assessment of Personality Through The Study of Mugs.* Yep, it certainly sounded good, far better than the topics she'd actually been given, which were so fascinating she couldn't even remember what they were. 'These two from the garden centre, one with the woman looking glamourous and sexy holding a trug of plums, well, that's obviously me! And the one with several chubby, homely looking women all serving teas in a marquee – is that what I'll grow into?' She smiled at her own joke. 'Maybe that's what I'm really like now, only just don't see it.' They'd said in a hairdressing lecture that when we look in a mirror, we see ourselves the way we were in our late twenties, not what the mirror really reflects, so who could say? 'Is that why photos are always such a shock?' she mused. 'And in years to come, when I see myself in a mirror, will I see myself as I am now? I really hope not!'

She picked up the one with the signs of the zodiac on it. That was a Christmas present. 'Now, if anyone saw it other than me,' she reasoned, 'they might think "this is a woman with an interest in the stars" whereas the reason I got it was that it was half price in the sale *(it said so on the label)* and Izzy was so broke it was all she could afford and I'm really, really touched that she wanted to give me a present at all, so I'm not going to throw it away, even though I think it's naff.'

An insistent cacophony of sounds disturbed the tranquillity of her thoughts. 'About time I changed that ring tone. It's been on the agenda for long enough.'

In two minds about whether or not she should answer it, she picked it up and stared at the screen. She could see it was her mother and wasn't at all sure she wanted another lengthy lecture about 'doing something about herself' and 'putting herself out there again.' She was a busy mum, looking after a small child and training for a career, one that she could fit round school hours, how much time did she have to primp and preen? 'Stop going to those silly W.I. meetings, then. You won't find another man there,' had been her mother's response when she'd pointed out the restrictions on her time. Little did her mother know that without those women at the WI, she couldn't begin to imagine how she'd have coped since Del did his disappearing act. 'And where is he, Lally? Have you made any effort to find out?' her mother kept asking. No, she wouldn't answer the phone right now. All that could wait.

She picked up the one that said 'The more people I meet, the more I love my cat.' She got that at a charity sale in the Town Hall for a quid. It made her laugh but she didn't really feel like that. She loved Mittens, of course. 'She's gorgeous, with a beautiful coat and a knowing look in her eyes' but she loved her friends, too, who'd stepped up for her in so many ways.

Mittens had arrived on the doorstep one day scrawny and with patchy fur and although Lally felt sorry for her, it was Chelsea's reaction that had sealed the deal. Somehow, the tiny toddler, only just starting to walk, managed to get Del's (uncooked) steak off the kitchen table and hand it over to the poor starving animal. Del wasn't best pleased, so Lally made it up to him by cooking a lemon meringue pie. 'Not really the same thing, babes,' he'd said to her. But all the same, he ate the lot in two sittings. Was that when things started to go wrong? How many little details were there that pointed in the direction of a marital crisis and she'd just never noticed them? 'Why won't men talk?' she asked herself for the hundredth time. They definitely hadn't covered that in the sixth form.

There were a few others trying to tell a story that no-one could really hear– the beautiful bird mugs Aunty Jane bought her before she died, the koala mug that cousin Joel brought back from Sydney, the Beatrix Potter that she got from Dolly when she went to the Lake District. They all mean something but it's difficult to know exactly what, beyond that she liked to have keepsakes of people – and things – that had meant a lot to her. Maybe that was it. Maybe these mugs simply told her 'People matter. Look after them as carefully as you do the mugs.'

Now, that was a piece of wisdom almost worthy of Mrs Khan.

AROMATHERAPY

Gos and Lally bumped into each other during Lally's search for Nilgiri tea and were enjoying a break in one of the posh cafes in the Mall.

'That must have been mum's idea,' said Gos. 'It's always been one of her favourites.'

He was right – she'd suggested they try it in their blends even though her own first attempt hadn't worked. Whilst Lally had never heard of it, Gos agreed that it was very good indeed. 'It's so difficult to find, I'd never have believed it existed if Mrs Khan hadn't shown me the packet,' she said. Then silently turning over in her mind whether or not she could ask him if Mrs Khan had a first name, she enquired instead 'Has your mother always been so keen on tea?' He'd suggested she let him treat them to coffee and cake – what else? – in return for a packet of the tea mix she and his mother came up with.

'She's always been a connoisseur of tea, obviously,' – *obviously? Thought Lally but didn't interrupt him* – 'and she's decided that creating the ultimate blend should be her entry on the bucket list,' he told her, doing his best to make their rendezvous last as long as he could.

'Ah, so she's thought of it too,' replied Lally. 'She's come up with some wonderful mixtures. The W.I. have been good at providing feedback. Maybe 'tea testing' should be one of the skills offered in the quarterly magazine.' Changing the subject completely: 'What made you come back?' she asked. When he'd left just before the Christmas break, he'd told her he wasn't intending to return until late spring or early summer. She'd seen him around for a few weeks now.

'Things didn't quite work out. I like it here. It'll be a wrench leaving the US but overall it's the way forward for me. A clean break.' He said nothing more about his absent wife or the place he'd called home for more than twenty years. Lally was learning from Mrs Khan's example that it could be infinitely better to wait for people to open up, rather than quiz them. She concentrated on the delicious aroma making its way to her nose from the coffee cup.

'Will you be looking for a house of your own?' she asked.

'Renting to start with. Mum's lovely but she's got a full life without looking out for me; and if I'm honest, I feel a bit crowded living in the house where I grew up.'

'When does the new job start?'

'Officially in the summer but unofficially I'm starting to prepare now. Another coffee?' he asked, willing her to say yes.

'Another time. I've got a lot on before I pick Chelsea up and I'm behind already. Thanks for the offer. I'll keep you to it.'

As she left the Mall, she felt sure she saw Di Lewis coming out of the Surgery looking very downcast. 'I wonder what's wrong?' she thought. But then 'How do you ask someone that self-contained if they want to bend your ear or not?' Slightly uncomfortable, she decided for the moment to leave well alone. She'd come up with a contingency plan in case it happened again.

***

The speaker that month, a young woman called Ceyda, had

brought a number of bottles containing various essences so the women could create perfumes for themselves. The results were variable, to put it kindly. In situations like these, Ceyda had learned the best thing to do was let them play. There were bound to be disasters but in the course of these talks, she'd come across some unusual combinations that might even have a future in the market with a bit of refinement. Not that she'd use them herself, of course, at least, not yet. Her company was tiny and they had no wish to grow. The personal touch was at the root of their success – too much growth and that would be lost.

'What got you into making perfumes in the first place?' Beth was intrigued. It wasn't something they came up with in careers sessions at school, not in her day anyway.

'It was my brother's doing, really. We were both out of work and he found a book in a charity shop on extracting essential oils from plants. He started playing around in his shed and it grew from there.'

'I never realised there was so much to it. Preparing everything from raw ingredients must mean that you have problems if crops fail. Have you got back up plans, you know, suppliers if you can't do the supplying yourself?' Beth was monopolising this Q and A session in the same way that Dr Di had earlier with Andrew. Jenny, standing in for Val, was thinking she would need to put the brakes on soon to give someone else a chance.

'We have to have plans in case of disasters like that, but so far, things have gone our way and we've not needed to use them. We extract and store a lot of the essences, so we don't really expect to run out of them, but it could happen. What has happened, though, is that we've sold every bottle of a particular blend when the demand has taken us by surprise in summer, and fortunately, customers have been very understanding. It's mercifully rare. We maintain large-ish stocks and keep a close eye on the day-to-day turnover, so we know what needs replenishing on a daily basis. As I explained earlier, the quickest one we've ever made was a rose based perfume that took just over three months, to a herby collection that took us over a year and we have to work with the natural cycle of things.'

Ceyda was used to these questions. The wording might be different, but we all like to know the same things when it comes down to it, so she had the answers at her finger-tips. Beth chipped in again: 'So you've never had to go to other nurseries ever?' Jenny decided this was beginning to sound more like interrogation and would step in once Ceyda had concluded her reply.

'Only for things we can't grow ourselves. With the bog standard produce, it's not happened yet but if we had to, then we'd approach one of the suppliers we have in our "emergency box",' she said, and before Beth could follow this up, Jenny butted in with 'Moira, you wanted to ask something?'

'So how many of you are there in the business?'

'Just the five of us: my brother and I, with him doing the horticulture and me concentrating on the blending and extraction. James, who's split half and half between grow-ing and manufacture and then there's Sally, who sources all the equipment and raw materials like rare plants our own nursery can't produce. Last but not least, we have Amara, who does all the admin work. He came to us on work experience and asked us if he could have a job. As soon as his GCSEs were finished, we took him on. We were lucky to find him.'

They could have continued with the questioning for hours but the feeling was that it should be continued over the cookery session. There was general agreement that it was an excellent afternoon and the suggestion was mooted that Ceyda should come back and do a full day workshop on a Saturday, when more women would be available. It would be perfect for Lally, most definitely, who'd been unable to get there and Di Lewis might even want to join in; and there were other women who would like to get stuck in again and make more. They'd put it in the suggestions book for the next W.I. year.

***

Val hadn't really enjoyed the cruise. She'd been quiet ever since their return and was longing to phone Mrs Khan and ask if they could meet. Seeing Gos and Lally in the coffee shop tipped her over into a decision. 'Mrs Khan, have you got time for a catch up any time soon?' she'd used her mobile phone. Best to do it before overthinking it caused her to change her mind.

'Of course. Would you like to come here or meet elsewhere?'

They arranged to meet at the seafront cafe next to the theatre.

***

'There's that man again,' thought Val. 'I wonder if he ever gets his hair cut.'

The Wizard looked lost in thought, like there was a lot more on his mind than the enormous slice of gateau he was ploughing his way through – it looked delicious and as usual, the portion was big enough for the whole town to have a share and still have some left over for the gulls.

'How was your holiday?' Mrs Khan wanted to know once they'd ordered their drinks.

'Fine.' Val was surprised that now they were together for a chat, the need to go into details or whinge about the experience was nowhere near as pressing.

'And Caribbean Sea and all that lies within it? Was it all you hoped it would be?'

'Yes and no. We didn't have enough time in any of the places we stayed. Martin and Miranda were obviously in the middle of a private row. Lawrence was short-tempered because he didn't like the heat and felt uncomfortable, having asked his friends to join us and finding that the atmosphere could be cut with a blunt buzz saw. I got a stomach upset.'

'Ah,' said Mrs Khan, 'maybe not so fine after all.'

'Mrs Khan, may I tell you the truth?'

'Of course. Why else bother to speak?'

'If Lally hadn't moved in to April Cottage, I'd probably go back,' Val was surprised at her own candour. 'Thank goodness for Lally,' thought Mrs Khan. 'Can't run away every time things don't go as we would like.' What she actually said was 'Maybe you are expecting a little too much too soon. The first flush is finished now. No longer the excitement of the early days, when love is all. Love is now backdrop and foundation for life, not total focus.'

'So it's not the beginning of the end after all,' thought Val. Why did things sound so sensible coming from Mrs K's mouth? 'I guess you're right,' she said, surprised for the second time that afternoon for toying with the idea of a snack. She'd eaten so much on the boat – or ship, as she was regularly reminded – she couldn't quite believe she'd want to cause her stomach any more suffering. But she felt safe in the presence of this enigma of a woman, like she could rely on wisdom that would be both straightforward and practical.

'Shall we go down to beach?' asked Mrs Khan, 'enjoy the sound of waves and the aroma of seaweed?'

They paid for their drinks and made their way along the seafront.

'We've come a long way,' thought Val, unaware that the same thought was passing through her friend's brain. 'What is it makes people think most complicated solution is always best solution?' Mrs Khan had deliberated on this many times before and found no satisfactory answer.

'Enjoy your marriage, Mrs Ford. It could come to an unexpected end and take you by surprise, unpleasant one, at that.'

Val was thoughtful on the way home. She hardly noticed the route she took or the people she passed, but was better disposed to Lawrence on her return, in spite of the fact that he'd burned the stew and sent out for a takeaway instead.

APRIL

TEDDY BEARS AND TV

You had to hand it to Helena. She really knew how to generate interest. This particular afternoon, she'd managed somehow to get a crew down from WestTime TV to cover Shelagh's Teddy Bears' Picnic in the Square. Although Shelagh was a member of the WI, this had not been on the Bucket List and she hadn't even considered asking for an entry on the grid. Her main contribution to the W.I. – as she saw it – was in helping to produce the newsletter, distributed free in shops. She really didn't have that much time for all this Bucket List malarkey and certainly didn't want any of the publicity that was following in its wake. Helena, however, was determined that the Stackton-on-Sea W.I. should get all the publicity they possibly could – not, you understand, publicity for herself. Shame on you for even thinking it!

***

Spring was well underway in Stackton, the days were longer and brighter and all those signs of hope and renewal associated with the season were in full force throughout the town. The time was right for something a little more weighty when the women met up again.

The talk that month had been informative and as far as possible, he'd made it amusing, 'but there aren't that many laughs available when talking about inescapable disease processes,' thought Mrs K. Not that they are necessarily inescapable, they'd learned. He'd been sure to emphasise that although you might have the genes, you won't automatically get the illness associated with them. It depended on all sorts of factors in both the interaction of the gene with other genes and the ongoing interaction between the genotype and the environment.

'So could you explain the difference between genotype and phenotype again, please?' asked Jenny.

'The genotype is what you inherit, the phenotype is what shows up in the organism,' he said.

'I guess ten year olds learn this in their science lessons these days,' thought Mrs Khan, 'but good few years since any of us was ten. Even Lally left that behind long ago.'

***

Shelagh had held these parties at the end of the summer term for all her classes throughout her entire career. It was one of the many reasons every child in the school looked forward to being in Mrs Buchanan's class. Sometimes, she missed those days and having pondered over the idea for far too long, had managed to get permission from the Residents' Association to hold the event, suggesting that they ask for donations to pay for things like plants and benches. Used to Risk Assessments, this one had been well prepared before she even took the idea to the meeting.

'I see you have provision here for thirty children and only two helpers. Do you really think that will be adequate,' asked the Committee's Jobsworth. The rest of the participants suppressed a groan. He had a point, they supposed.

'Children will be accompanied by parents and carers. There'll be lots more people helping out than are detailed on the plan.'

'And what about safeguarding?' asked Mr Jobsworth, looking over the top of his glasses. 'Why does he bother to do that?' thought Shelagh. 'If he doesn't need them, why doesn't he just take them off?' But what she said was 'The assistants and I all have clearance. I can't speak for the parents but I'm guessing they didn't bother to be vetted before they had the kids in the first place.' She hoped her irritation wasn't showing. This sort of thing was a con- tributor to her decision to take early retirement while she was still loving the core of the work. Better to go out on a high, she thought, than get jaded like so many of them did.

'I think we've heard enough now,' said Jobsworth's wife. 'Shelagh's obviously done loads of this sort of thing and the Risk Assessment explains everything clearly, if we take the time to read it carefully.' Jobsworth looked less than happy. 'So I suggest we put it to the vote.' It was passed unanimously and Shelagh set to with getting it organised.

***

'So what you all need to know is that the Stackton W.I. is a very dynamic organisation. We do loads to support each other as well as having a really entertaining and informa- tive programme. And of course, we have the Bucket List.'

Shelagh felt that Helena had somewhat hijacked the afternoon but she didn't really care. There was so much more interest now that the TV crew were in the Square.

It'd sold out completely and the children – and their cuddly companions – were having a delightful time. Once the TV crew turned up, though, there'd been a veritable swarming of visitors, with hefty donations going in the box. The Committee couldn't complain now. There must be a few hundred quid in there.

Even Jobsworth had raised a smile or two. 'Please don't let the TV crew interview him,' thought Shelagh, as, indeed, did Mrs Jobsworth. He was pompous enough already, without turning him into a Television Star as well. In the event, the only person they were really interested in was Helena, who was doing a wonderful PR job, and although they weren't allowed to film the children or carers, the Teddy Bears were shown having a truly wonderful time.

***

'And of course, the Bucket List has been one of the best new innovations of the season. Next year, we're going to try to get a team on *Eggheads*.'

Forty pairs of eyebrows shot up simultaneously, perfectly synchronised with the dropping of jaws. The word had quickly been passed round that Helena was going to be on the local news that evening and they'd all tuned in. No-one had heard of this plan before today and they wondered what else she had up her sleeve, but there were no more surprises in store before the broadcast ended.

'Thank heaven for that,' thought Mrs Khan. 'She'd have us all on International Space Station if she thought it would forward her quest to make us famous.'

Some of the women liked the idea of a W.I. appearance on *Eggheads*, so who knows what would find its way on to next year's Bucket List?

***

The Wizard was impressed. 'She sure has got something,'

he thought. 'You can't take your eyes off her.' Charisma. She knew how to command attention all right, and with no apparent effort in doing so. He'd have to get moving with his plans before someone else moved in on her.

***

Not everyone was quite as pleased. Since Helena's bombshell about *Eggheads*, Val had received nearly a hundred and fifty enquiries about joining the WI. True, most of them – one hundred and twenty nine – had been within the first twenty four hours, but word was still getting around. At this rate, they were going to have to form another sub-Committee to deal with all the requests.

'I wish she'd think before she opens her mouth,' she told Lawrence, closing the computer.

'She probably did and got the exact response she was hoping for. Most of them won't follow through but it'll give you new blood and all sorts of fresh ideas.' Val didn't look convinced. He continued 'You're always saying it gets more and more difficult every year to come up with ideas for interesting programmes. An influx of members could help with that.'

Val relented slightly but thought of all the extra work and decided it really was time to let someone else take over the reins. She'd had a wonderful time but at the end of the season, she'd be ready to move on.

PROGRAMMES

'The History of the Teapot,' thought Mrs Khan. 'Very worthy topic but I can't imagine Stackton-on-Sea programming such a meeting.' She stopped short of thinking she couldn't quite believe anyone sane in the whole country would put it in – she wasn't that type of woman. Still, she shouldn't be criticising if she couldn't think of anything for the suggestions box herself. One problem was that it was only April and the new season wouldn't be starting until September, another five months away. So much time for things to change. It had to be done though and they should all do their best. 'When all said and done,' she decided, 'WI is responsibility of all. Can't criticise if we don't play our part.' Best not to criticise at all, she added.

***

Val and Gina were rehearsing all day with the choir, and as Mrs Khan was out with Gos, the three of them missed the outing to Stratford-upon-Avon.

'Is this really happening?' Maureen had been blown away by the enthusiastic response to Mrs Khan's suggestion that they make the annual W.I. Day Out a visit to Stratford for the weekend of Shakespeare's birthday. Gos had been years ago before he moved to the USA. They'd talked about it since and she'd passed the information on. It was going to be expensive, that much was clear, but what a way for Maureen to get her tick on the grid!

***

Maureen was, in fact, in danger of bubbling over. She'd loved the play – *Cymbeline*, not one she knew or had even heard of – but so exciting. A really interesting piece of theatre; and all those famous faces from the box right there in front of her, so different from the way they appeared on the small screen and so skilled! How did they do it? she wondered. 'How many of these young actors who no-one really knows about now will be household names in five years' time?' She had so many questions but no-one to get the answers from. 'And which ones will they be?' Her own favourite had been the bloke with the blond curly hair who did the singing. She knew that piece, not well of course, but it was quite famous. *Fear no more the heat of the sun.* Yep. She liked the sentiments expressed in that. She thought she might ask for it to be sung at her own funeral but there was time to think about that later. Much later. At the moment, all she wanted was to soak up the atmosphere.

The hotel was small but very comfortable and when they got back after the show, they had the lounge more or less to themselves. There were only two other residents there, a couple of distinguished looking men drinking shorts from the bar and chatting amiably before turning in for the night.

'Hi Ladies,' one of them called over, 'taken in a show?' It wasn't clear who should be answering, so Maureen herself piped up: 'Yes. My first time in Stratford. We've been to see *Cymbeline*'

'Enjoy it?' asked the other one, appearing genuinely interested.

'Oh yes! This is my dream of a lifetime.' She told him all about the W.I. Bucket List and her wish to see a Shakespeare play here in Stratford. Intrigued, he asked a number of follow up questions.

'Coming back?' he wanted to know when they'd finished discussing the ins and out of the W.I. and its aspirations.

'I really hope so. It's been wonderful.'

Kathy asked the barman to take a picture of the whole group, including their two new, albeit fleeting friends, with which request he duly obliged.

Watching the procession on Saturday morning, Maureen turned to a woman behind her in the crowd and asked 'Do you know who those two men are?' She learned that they were Richard Keenlyside and Alex Anderson, two of the lead actors in one of the other plays and they'd been enjoying a quiet evening in their hotel away from the crowds. Wow, now that was something to put in the family archive.

Kathy's husband had driven them up in the transit van on Friday afternoon and he'd be taking them home after lunch. No-one had a clue where he was now.

Watching the procession, Maureen was quite impressed at the variety of locals taking part in the festivities. All the actors from the show they'd seen the previous evening (and all the other shows, she suspected); local dignitaries, children from the primary schools – so many different groups were parading through the town with banners to honour the Immortal Bard. Bringing up the rear were the Stratford-upon-Avon Morris dancers, all kitted out and doing their best to dance their way round the town. Maureen had never realised how sexy they were before this morning (*I'm*

tempted to ask if any of us ever has but I'm trying to learn from Mrs Khan and not be quite so sceptical...... note from author).
She turned to Beth and Jenny 'Wouldn't it be nice if we had something like this in Stackton, something to bring all the different community groups together.' 'I suppose there's the Bridgwater Carnival,' said Jenny. 'But it's not really local to us, is it,' added Beth. 'Put it to the Bucket List Committee in the summer,' she suggested. 'Now, there's an idea,' thought Maureen. 'If we could find someone to organise it, naturally. I wonder if Mrs Khan would be interested.'

***

'What about *One hundred and One Ways with a Paper Bag?*' suggested Gos.

'You're being very naughty,' replied Mrs K. 'WI programme is important. If we don't get it right, women won't come.' Gos doubted that very much. It seemed to him that they came for much more than the stimulation of an interesting speaker. 'Why don't I suggest you talk to us about your research?' she asked.

'Don't think so, mum. I'll be in my new job by then. Don't want to go missing as soon as I arrive.' This wasn't quite true but Gos had the good sense to know he didn't have the right touch to engage such a diverse collection of lively women. He'd grown fond of his mother's W.I. friends. Besides, he knew how much comfort she'd derived from them after his dad died.

'Well, what about *The Significance of the Internal Combustion Energy in Psychotherapy*? You could invite Amir over to give that one,' he said.

'Are you mocking your brother?' asked Mrs K, smiling all the same.

171

'Heaven forbid!' The two men were about as alike as a plant pot and a fountain pen but they got on well and neither minded being teased by the other.

'Maybe get someone in to talk about reduced life expectancy related to being mother of two sons', said Mrs Khan, affectionately looking up at Gos.

'Now you're talking,' he said, guiding her into a café. 'Let's drink to that.'

***

Back in Stratford, they were making the most of lunch before embarking on the journey home. There'd not been a great deal of time for sightseeing and none at all for looking round the gift shops. Maureen didn't care. She had last night's programme and knew she'd treasure it forever. Hers had been a really modest entry on the Bucket List compared with some, but it was something that had grown and grown. She'd never forget it.

Piling into the transit, she was convinced she'd caught a glimpse of Dr Di and the man she was with reminded her of that Andrew, the one who did the talk and strutted his stuff at Helena's Christmas show. Surely that couldn't be the case! If there was something going on, it would have got out. In a place like Stackton, where people knew and looked out for each other, it would have been noticed, surely, and there were plenty of gossipmongers around. She felt slightly embarrassed at that thought. Wasn't she thinking gossip herself, even if she wasn't speaking it? Still, it'd be interesting to know. She'd be sure to keep her ears and eyes open. That'd be an outcome from the Bucket List nobody could have entered on the grid. Did accidentals count?

***

At home in the Khan household that night, Gos disappeared to take a phone call. From the tone of his voice, it was clearly very strained. When he went back into the living room, his face was a bit like a popped balloon and all the good humour of the day had evaporated.

"Night mum.' And with that he went to bed and left her wondering.

SWELL WOOD

'Are you sure we're on the right road, my love?' Lawrence was querying Val's skills as a navigator, not for the first time. 'You've said before you've never really been much cop at reading a map.' The satnav wasn't working.

Val was doing everything she could to incorporate herself fully into Lawrence's world. To be fair, it wasn't much of a hardship. She liked his friends and found the goings-on in the orchestra intriguing. For his part, Lawrence thought he should do more to learn about the things that had occupied her in the days before they met. Between them they concluded that they should try more wildlife watching together, as that had been her true passion, albeit sadly neglected since their nuptials. He really didn't want to join the WI, though she'd told him often enough that he could.

To start off their programme of events, they settled on Swell Wood. In spite of all the volunteering she'd done with the Trust, Val had never been there and she understood that the heronry was quite something. Mrs Khan had visited several times and spoken really highly of it. Birdwatching was up there with her love of gardening. 'You'll love it,' she'd told them. 'This must be Best County in whole world for discovery of nature.' So far, she'd been right.

Lawrence refused point blank to replace the faulty satnav claiming that ownership of such a device causes the user to lose all sense of direction and time. Maybe he's right, thought Val, but at least you get where you want to be and the person with the map doesn't end up with earache.

It has to be admitted that they'd been on the road for a ridiculously long time. The interweb said it would take thirty five minutes and the journey had so far taken an hour and forty.

'I'm doing my best,' said Val, 'but you're right, we don't seem to be making much headway.'

Lawrence stopped the car and took the map. 'I think I can see where things have gone slightly awry,' he said and in spite of doing his very best to be patient and under-standing, the expression on his face stated clearly 'why am I driving through the Somerset countryside with my map-blind wife in the adjacent seat, who by her own admission can't navigate her way out of a crisp packet and has no interest in learning?'

'We're supposed to be going north along this road, only you have the map upside down, which means we're driv-ing south. Instead of turning left at the junction, you told me to turn right.' Ah. He was being absolutely sure that there was no doubt with whom the problem lay. Well, she'd repeated over and over again that reading a map had never been among her strong points, in spite of doing geography A' level. 'It's not really a skill they teach you,' she thought. It was all *Peach Canning in Australia* and *How to Recognise Sedimentary Rock,* rather than the Brighton variety, she supposed; and ever since the satellite system had been in place, she'd not even attempted to work out routes for herself.

To continue: with great forbearance, Lawrence made the executive decision to find somewhere local to have a coffee and discuss if they wanted to continue on their quest to find Swell Wood today. If they decided to make the attempt again, they could draw up one of those Idiot's Guides by studying the web pages – you know the sort of thing, 'turn left at the *Lady Windermere's Fan*, drive for half a mile, go round the Big Roundabout to the Second Exit (the one with the Corner Shop Selling Everything Bar The One Thing You Really Need) and keep going until you get to a bridge with pictures of the Twelve Days of Christmas painted on it in luminous green...' You've probably engaged with this sort of fool proof itinerary yourself.

Over coffee and yet another cake – a sedate affair with Lawrence visibly trying to calm himself with every bite and sip – he asked. 'And you're sure Mrs Khan said that we're going at the right time of year?'

'Yes, Lawrence,' replied Val, herself a little irritated at this point. 'The heronry's there for a few weeks from April to sometime in June. She said that if we come now, we can observe the birds getting bigger as the nesting season progresses.'

'Right. Well, let's have another look.'

Lawrence had taken the map and was studying it extremely carefully.

'It's not that far from Glastonbury. I vote we get back there (*they'd already passed Glastonbury once that morning but it wasn't* quite *as close as he thought*) have some lunch and then take a detailed look at the map so that we get there this afternoon.'

***

'I know you don't like this town,' said Val, 'but it was your idea to come.' They'd both forgotten that Tuesday was market day and parking spots were not that easy to come by. On the plus side, there was a herb stall selling some really interesting plants, so if they could ever escape the confines of the car, there would be some sterling additions to the garden.

'Only because it's close to Swell Wood.' Lawrence was beginning to wish he'd never suggested this trip out at all but that they'd stayed in bed instead.

'Well, shall we go home, sort out an itinerary and try again tomorrow?'

'No!' Lawrence almost shouted. He'd spotted a car leaving the big car park and if he was nifty, could get in there and finally stretch his legs. He was firmly of the resolve never to even use the words Swell Wood again after today, let alone repeat the attempt to find the wretched place.

Lunch was tasty, albeit a little strained. Val suggested they separate for half an hour or so and have a look around the shops. Eager to get a bit of space and regain his composure, Lawrence agreed.

By the time they got back into the car, Lawrence was again a vision of serenity, having purchased some excellent provisions from the local bakery, ostensibly to save Val from having to bake but really because she didn't make this sort of cake. He'd also carefully studied how to proceed with the journey. Val had popped into a couple of charity shops and bought herself some very interesting clothes. Glastonbury being Glastonbury, there were things there she'd never seen anywhere else ever. She was pleased with her acquisitions.

'Right. I've written the directions down. Could you read them to me as we go along?'

'No problem.' Surely that would be easy enough. Or would it?

In the event, the route was so picturesque that Val kept forgetting to look at the sheet he'd prepared for her, so by the time she informed him he was supposed to turn left (or right, as the case may be) he'd already passed the turning. This meant either a U-turn or waiting until they reached a roundabout, with the ensuing necessity for Val to then recognise the point at which she would have to say left instead of right. Confused? So was she. You really don't need to know the details of this trek but let's just say it didn't go well. 'Damn Mrs Khan,' thought Lawrence, 'and damn these b****** herons,' only then realised that without Mrs Khan, he'd never have met Val in the first place, so silently relented.

By some uncanny stroke of luck and with absolutely no warning, there was a signpost upon which 'Swell Wood' was very clearly painted. 'Why the blazes couldn't they have done that before?' thought Lawrence, appreciating that he'd never know the answer.

They arrived feeling slightly better than they thought they might, having at least found the place. There was no-one else there if the car park was anything to go by, and they made their way up the trail set for visitors to the heronry. There was a sign pointing to a hide, so they took the short walk there, watching from the window and taking in the lush greenery and springtime awakening of the woods

Above them, balanced on the boughs of the trees were basket-like structures with herons sitting on their precious eggs, dozens of them, whichever way they looked. They stood for a few moments transfixed, peering up at the branches covered in perfectly constructed nests. The air was fresh and cool; and just visible through gaps in the trees they could see blue sky with only the occasional cloud. It was surprisingly quiet, allowing them to hear with great clarity the occasional snatches of assorted bird song. Val wanted to suggest that it might be the time of day when they all took a nap but thought better of it, realising it would only disturb the peace.

They sat there arm in arm, united in the spectacle of the moment. Even the soft sound of footsteps on the leaves outside didn't disturb them and when the hide door opened, they both turned to greet the newcomer.

'Afternoon,' he said. 'Herons behaving?'

'Oh yes,' answered Val. 'Apart from rookeries, I've never seen so many nests and honestly, who'd have thought they'd be so peaceful and accepting of one another!'

'First time?' asked the newcomer.

'Yes, it is,' she replied.

'First of many?' he asked.

'Oh yes,' said Lawrence, the trials of the drive there totally forgotten.

'Ay. Once you've seen it, you have to see it again and again,' said the newcomer. 'Glorious place, this,' he said and settled down next to the two of them with his binoculars. They sat there in silence for the best part of an hour.

**

Neither of them spoke on the way home. Leaving the wood behind had been a wrench but it'd taken so long to find it, the light was fading and they hadn't wanted to walk back to the car in the dark. It was a thirty minute drive from door to door.

'Another trip in four weeks?' said Lawrence, 'see how many of the babies have hatched?'

'Oh yes. Please!'

It was duly marked on the calendar and in bed that night, processing the events of the day, each decided that it had been worth all the little mishaps. They'd loved the woods and had discovered that the odd tiff does nothing to shake the foundations of a good relationship. In fact, given the nature of the activity taking place over the next hour or so, it might even be said to help to strengthen it.

MAY

THE ESTUARY

Galvanised by the talk on estuarine life, Mrs K had purchased a couple of identification guides from the local Wildlife Trust shop. The afternoon was so beautiful, she called Lally and asked if Chelsea would like a walk along the marshes.

As it happened, when he learned that Lally would be going too, even Gos managed to put his work away for the afternoon and joined them with a spring in his step. There'd been no more phone calls for a good while and his mood had lifted, whilst he was still clearly lower in mood than Mrs K would have liked. It was this unexpected outing with Lally and Chelsea that inspired the smile he was now wearing broadly.

'Marram grass,' said Gos, standing beside metres high rushes, some of which were taller than he was himself.

'Nonsense, my boy,' retorted his mother. 'Phragmites.' Looking unconvinced, he relented, not wishing to argue in front of the others. The afternoon was beginning to be fun.

***

'So why is it there are fewer winter birds on the marshes than there used to be?' asked Fiona on one of her rare visits to the Hut. The talk had been really engaging and had thrown up as many questions as it had answered. Jenny was unfailingly surprised to learn there was so much more to absolutely everything than met the eye.

'So many different possibilities. It could be that now the climate has warmed, they don't need to fly as far south as they used to. And then there are all the other things we touched on in the talk, like so-called sports shooting, falling brood sizes etc. If you'd like to discuss it further, please catch hold of me during the break.'

'The two birds you said are the only ones that eat the same diet, could you remind me what they were?' Dr Di, too, had found it more interesting than she thought she would.

'Brent geese and wigeon. Shall I put the slides up again?' and so saying, the excellent speaker showed the women the birds in question.

'I think we'd better make that the last one. If anyone wants to ask anything further, you'll have to catch Ruth over tea and cake.'

The tea was another blend prepared by Lally and Mrs K. Lally had been giving herself to the mission heart and soul, starting by getting books from the library and currently finding out where to source different teas without having to buy supermarket blends. She was surprised to discover just how many different types there were and how involved the whole process was. If they were both thinking of taking it seriously, she needed to know all these things. It was doing her good to have something new to do, particularly as Mrs Khan seemed to know quite a lot and was proving an excellent teacher.

***

'Which one's which, Ganny K?' asked Chelsea. Mrs Khan patiently pointed out the different wildfowl on the marsh. The bag of duck food had been exhausted some time ago and Lally and Gos had gone off on their own for a bit. Mrs Khan gave them her silent blessing, whilst not wishing to push things. In the first place, she had no proof that her younger son's marriage was over; and in the second, she knew better than to take up the post of matchmaker. She'd not let anyone do it for her.

'Where are the wiggly wormies, Ganny K?

'They're under the mud. We can't see them because they live there in secret, eating all the tiny little things that are too small for us to see.' Chelsea was so wrapped up in her quest to discover everything she could about the life of the estuary, she declined even the offer of an ice cream. Maybe Lally was right – she could be destined to become a naturalist. She was a lively child, outgoing and fun. So different from the way Gos had been – serious, thoughtful. Mrs K had worried about him sometimes, never seeming to have many friends, preferring his own company and his books. Amir was quite different – mischievous, naughty – but let's get back to the matter in hand.

When every possibility had been exhausted in Chelsea's not inconsiderable brain, Mrs Khan called Gos's mobile phone and arranged to meet him and Lally in the chip shop. After a slow stroll, they settled down to a plate of chips and cans of pop – not the ideal drink, they knew, but the two women could no longer tolerate substandard tea and this particular shop didn't run to proper coffee.

***

Lally wondered if this is how Dorothy felt when she was immersed in her chocolate making. It was a different world entirely and not just a matter of the variety of leaves. There was all the business of different soil types and climates, how they were grown and harvested – she imagined that cocoa bean growing must at least be as complex, if not more. She'd have to ask. Dorothy would be moving towards expert status now she was looking for a plantation to visit.

Of course, Lally's mother wasn't so keen on her new passion.

'Eulalia,' she'd started, as she walked through the front door of April Cottage. 'Exactly what do you think you're doing? When Del comes back, he's not even going to know where you are, and now you've let that man move in to your house! Well, what's he going to think?'

'You know what, mum, I don't honestly care. He walked out and left me alone with Chelsea, the daughter who adores him and whom he was supposed to adore in return. Gos pays my half of the mortgage so that I can afford to do the things for Chelsea I want to do. We've got lots of room here and she's happy.'

'It's disgraceful. You've made no attempt to find him and to even a casual observer, you've given up on your marriage. You took him until death you do part.'

'So did he.' Lally once again thought it better not to remind her mother that she, too, had suffered a broken marriage. 'Besides, I made every attempt, mum. He switched his phone off and it's not been back on since the day he failed to return from work. The only proof I have he's still alive is his monthly transfer into the bank account, which only just covers Chelsea's basic needs and keeps a roof over her head. Do you want me to get a private detective on to him?'

'Now you're being silly, Eulalia. You always were prone to flights of fancy and you've obviously not grown up in that sense, either. But honestly, what with your clear abandonment of your marriage and now this tea blending nonsense on top of the hairdressing! Whatever next? Have you got any idea what people think?'

If truth be told, Lally cared even less about what people thought than she did about the history of knicker elastic (one of the topics suggested – and mercifully rejected – for next year's W.I. programme) but couldn't be bothered to argue. She'd done a good job of adjusting to her changed circumstances and made every effort to make Chelsea's life happy and stable. If her mother didn't like it, tough. She'd either have to learn to live with it or butt out of Lally's life altogether.

***

Gos had returned with his mother and they were now sitting in her back garden, a favourite venue for both. The spring garden was especially pleasing this year, what with all the birds that had chosen this personal patch of greenery to set up their nests.

'It's lovely here, mum,' he said, sipping a gin and tonic. 'You've kept it beautifully. Dad would have been proud.'

'Of you too, son,' she replied.

Mother and son sat in companionable silence until long after the sun had gone down.

'Wonderful,' thought Mrs Khan. 'Many nights now warm enough to watch stars and drink tea.'

***

In the garden of April Cottage, Lally was doing and thinking the same thing, while Chelsea was sleeping soundly with her wiggly worm toy resting on the pillow. What would she do if Del turned up again? It was perfectly possible he might. 'Cross that bridge when we come to it,' she decided.

What a difference a year makes.

OF G-STRINGS AND MEMORIES

Mrs Khan was not having the best of days.

She wore a sari on only three days of the year: her wedding anniversary, her late husband's birthday and to commemorate the day he departed this world. This particular occasion was the last mentioned and she was wearing the emerald green with the gold thread. It was beautiful and elegant, as are most saris, but not practical in Stackton-on-Sea and as there are many lovely clothes in the Western tradition, she was very happy to conform to local sartorial norms.

Moving from the kitchen to her bedroom carrying a large pile of ironed clothing, she tripped over Tigger. Not being the sort of person to utter oaths, she simply let out a gasp of both horror and exasperation. The sari, being slippery, got in the way when she tried to get up and she was therefore obliged to make a number of attempts, finally removing it and kicking it as far as she could so that she could pull herself upright again. She decided against replacing the offending item of clothing with something similar and dressed instead in a long, flowing skirt with a colourful, lightweight sweater.

Deciding to call in at the chemist to get some ointment to rub on the knee she'd knocked in the rather minor incident, she stopped at a zebra crossing for the usual purpose – to wait until the road was clear before crossing it.

'Here you are, dear, let me give you a hand.' She found her elbow being grabbed by a gentleman approximately twice her age who appeared to be considerably less mobile than she was herself; and being propelled across the road, having to dodge traffic in the process. As she recognised that his intention was kind and he was doing his best to help, she turned and thanked him, although her heart wasn't really in it.

On reaching her turn in the queue and making the appropriate enquiry, her ears were assailed with 'Mr Davies,' (being yelled by the assistant – about fifteen years old and quite possibly on work experience, thought Mrs Khan, attempting to be charitable but not being as successful as she would have liked) 'there's an old lady here had a fall and wants something for her knee.'

'At what point in life,' thought Mrs Khan, 'do we stop living our lives and find it happens to us? Most of my days on this earth, I would have fallen over. Now, quite suddenly, I have a fall. A few years ago, I could have waited perfectly happily at crossing until road was safe to cross. Now I have to be dragged across it by someone who would probably be better off being led by me and risk meeting my end under the wheels of an approaching car.'

Recognising that she was probably a little low at the sadness of the event she was honouring, she tried doing some slow breathing and thinking about the happy times she'd spent with the late Mr Khan.

However, as she wasn't concentrating on where she was going, she bumped into a total stranger, causing him to drop the several packages he was balancing in his arms. I won't tell you what he said to her – suffice it say it wasn't that polite.

'Should have had gnome repaired after all' she said to herself with a twinkly eye. 'Best to go home and do something useful there before whole of Stackton is wrecked by my ineptitude and neglect of duty in getting Mr Gnome's arm glued back on.' So saying, she made her way back and was silently relieved to be in her own private place of refuge.

***

Val, on the other hand, was feeling quite chuffed. She'd made her first ever golden syrup cake and – although she said so herself when she knew it was immodest – it had turned out excellent.

'Mrs Khan,' she said when the phone was picked up, 'would you like to come over for a cuppa and a slice of cake?'

'I would love to, Mrs Ford,' she said, 'but have a sore knee. I fell *no falls here, she thought,* and banged it against the wall. If you are so disposed, you are very welcome here.'

The afternoon saw the two friends chatting and laughing, pondering on the sudden change that occurs when a person acquires grey hairs or slows down in one's gait.

'It's not the change in us that's important per se. It's the way we're perceived,' offered Valerie. 'It's a cliché to say we feel the same inside, but it's so true. The other day, I was on the phone to the bank and the woman at the call centre said she had my details on the screen and asked if I'd like the number of the special helpline for the elderly in case I have to call again.'

'Should have told her about W.I. Bucket List,' said Mrs Khan.

'I told her I was thinking of joining a burlesque class,' said Valerie. 'It didn't take long after that to get the conversation back to the entries on my statement that had nothing to do with my spending habits.'

'Maybe an invitation to Middle Eastern Dance course W.I. is holding in summer would have been in order. She could have come and enjoyed it also, observed with her own eyes that getting older is not a punishment but a joy.'

When they'd exhausted the topic of *How the World Treats Me Now I'm Not Seventeen Anymore* – 'we could include in next year's W.I. programme, along with how we deal with personal response' said Mrs Khan – and Val had returned to Bayfield, she settled down to do some harp playing. She blessed the day she'd been brave enough to write to the Bristol Symphonic and they'd put her in touch with Lawrence. It really wasn't an exaggeration to say that that email had touched many lives.

She was improvising some gentle, ethereal music when the G-4 string broke. As we know, Mrs K is not one to utter oaths, so she simply went to the relevant drawer and looked for a replacement string. When she discovered she didn't have the right one – every other G string but not that – she alighted on the idea of calling Lawrence to ask if he could lend her one until she could order a replacement to arrive through the post.

'Bother,' she said (out loud, so she must have been feeling pretty put out). 'Valerie said he's on three-tier day and that tomorrow they're going to reserve at Ham Wall. I'll have to phone up early in morning and see if they can send one urgently.'

The rest of the evening was spent with her and Tigger reminiscing about the days of yore, Tigger purring loudly enough to deter the most determined of burglars while curled up in a ball on her lap. By the time she retired for the night, she'd done enough remembering of the past and looked forward to a new day tomorrow and, inevitably, another fresh adventure.

THE W.I. BUCKET LIST

'Okay ladies,' –

'Excuse me, madam President, we're not called ladies anymore. We're women now.' The not-so-new-anymore member, Bryony, seemed to be keen on political correctness. 'Good for her,' thought Val, 'but maybe the odd bit of give and take wouldn't be too bad a thing.' What she said was 'Okay, fellow members of the WI, shall we get going with the meeting now?'

The chatter died down. Val was definitely not going to miss this job in the future, even though Lawrence was urging her to think carefully before making it official.

'Mrs Khan didn't want to be part of the forward planning. She asked me to apologise on her behalf but said she's too busy with other things.' There was a low murmuring in the hall.

'Can I just say that I think we all appreciate the part she plays in the W.I. and the inspirational role she's had over the past two or three years?' Kathy was keen there should be sufficient acknowledgement of all Mrs Khan had contributed to the Stackton-on-Sea WI. The feeling of the meeting was with her.

'Okay. Let's put it in the minutes. How about treating her to something, flowers or chocolates?' Val thought this might be a bit boring but on the spur of the moment could come up with nothing more exciting.

'We can decide on that once we've sorted out how we're going to proceed,' suggested Jenny, the ideal person to take over in Val's opinion, but it wasn't her decision to make.

'So, let's get on with it. First things first. We're going to need loads of helpers for Di Lewis's sports day. There's a list up on the notice board. Fill in your details before you go, if you can. Next, how do we document and publicise what we've done so far?' With that, she handed over to Kathy, who'd been drawing up a plan.

***

Mrs Khan was both mystified and gratified that the Bucket List was going to continue into Year Two. She'd had no entry on the first one, having started to learn the harp well before its official instigation; and wasn't sure she'd want one in the future, in spite of her thoughts regarding tea blending. For all that, it was good to see how her friends and colleagues were pulling together to make their dreams come true. 'Maybe my dream should be to find space in garden for apple tree, even one of those tall spindly articles would do. They take up so little space. Could put picture of Amir's face on top and chat to him in the evening...' She'd give it some serious thought.

***

With Mrs Khan officially absent, there was no-one to take charge of the tea and coffee, to say nothing of the inevitable and absolutely essential cake. 'Should we make her Refreshments Officer? Officially, like President and Vice-President?' Helena was a little frustrated by the fact that the participants in the current gathering were less than keen on her idea of getting WestTime TV down to do a feature on them, but no matter. She'd find a way.

'Do we need a Refreshments Officer?' asked Bryony. It was good to have a new, young member and the women were doing their best to be open-minded, but she could appear a little humourless at times. Still, we all have our less appealing characteristics so she had to be allowed hers.

'Probably not,' replied Beth, 'but she and Lally do a large amount to keep us fed and watered; and they're working on the W.I. Tea Blend, so it might be nice to acknowledge the work they put in.' In reality, Beth had more commitment to the idea of disembowelling herself with a toothpick than adding another member to the W.I. hierarchy; but there was something about this young woman she simply couldn't get along with and was enjoying contradicting her. The other women were beginning to notice. Bryony just sniffed. As long as she had the opportunity to make her point, she didn't mind what the outcome was. She was happy just to be heard.

'Okay, let's put it to the vote. Do we want an official Refreshments Officer or not?'

As it turned out, Mrs Khan was voted in and with the exception of Bryony, who abstained, there was complete agreement.

'Good grief,' thought Val, 'am I really party to this?' Her circumstances had changed beyond all recognition and she was getting increasingly enthusiastic about throwing herself as fully as she could into her life with Lawrence. She'd even been asking him about music degrees – not that he knew anything, of course. It was the best part of half a century since he'd done any training; but he was doing his best to help her expand her knowledge and under-standing. 'I think I'll tell them today I'm going. Might as well get it over with,' she decided. 'Not just the Bucket List that needs updating.'

***

Dorothy was minding Chelsea for the afternoon. Having not yet completed her entry on this year's List and not being at all sure she really wanted one for next season, she couldn't see any point in being at the meeting.

Chelsea was a strange little girl, Dorothy decided. She'd offered her the chance to make chocolates and eat as many as she wanted but instead, Chelsea elected to go in the garden and look for weeds and insects. She was perfectly content trotting around the flower beds seeing what she could find, pulling up the odd weed – after checking, naturally – and getting as many plants identified as she could. 'I don't think it would have been my choice when I was four,' thought Dorothy. 'What a sweet, undemanding child.'

When Lally picked her up at 6 o'clock, she was delighted to learn that Chelsea had behaved impeccably and that she and Dorothy had had such a lovely time together. She wasn't doing such a bad job after all, even though her mother and sister had spent the afternoon trying to convince her she was.

***

'Right, my man,' said Mrs Khan, carefully laying all the pieces out on the bench in the shed. 'Time to get you well again.' Gos had offered to effect the repair but she wouldn't hear of it. After all, he thought she should put Mr Gnome in the dustbin –'He's the best part of forty years old, mum, and you never liked him anyway.' – and he might not be as committed to restoring the health of her ceramic protector as she was herself. 'He's part of your heritage, son,' she said. 'Something for the grandchildren to cherish.' Gos doubted that – so did she, but what's the odd white lie between mother and son?' – but he let her get on with it. It was her home and her property, so hardly his call.

She was very careful to use the right glue and to be sure that all the parts were spotlessly clean before attempting to assemble them. Painstakingly, she did everything on the instruction leaflet that came with the tube and left him overnight to dry out fully.

'Apart from odd chip and big chunk missing from shoulder joint, you could be young man again,' she told him, placing him carefully in his old dwelling place to the right of the front door. 'I rely on you to ensure no more "falls", no more well-meaning but infirm elderly gentlemen doing their best to get me run over; no more visits to chemist to be humiliated by kind but misguided twelve year olds behind counter,' she thought, going back into the house. 'A good day's work.' She closed the door and forgot all about him for the time being, feeling pleased with a job well done.

***

After a great deal of debate – virtually all of it totally unnecessary, in Val's opinion – decisions were made.

Kathy and Jenny were going to prepare a free newsletter to distribute round the town's café's, library and shops informing the populace, both permanent and temporary, of the events of the last year and what the women had achieved. Various members were going to make contributions.

Moira was going to prepare a completed grid to display on the W.I. Hut notice board. Both of these innovations were to be in place by the time the summer fair took place. So far, so good.

The more difficult decisions related to the coming year. Val throwing a spanner in the works with her announcement hadn't helped matters but she was unwilling to take full responsibility. Maureen's insistence that they should do their best to get a Stackton-on-Sea Carnival on the agenda had divided opinion and some of the debate had been quite heated. Finally, they'd decided that Kathy (again) would buy a book and anyone wanting to be placed on the official list would be able to make their own entry, one per page, telling what they wanted to do, along with requests for helpers, if such were needed. The fly in the ointment buzzed into the room when Bryony said she wanted to be responsible for preparing next year's grid and keeping it updated. No-one could be quite sure if this was because she genuinely wanted to integrate more fully into the life of the W.I. or simply that she wanted to get up Beth's nose. Sentiments were divided approximately equally but no-one voiced them either way.

***

'At least buying Mrs Khan a garden centre voucher proved to be uncontentious,' Val informed Lawrence over dinner that evening.

'You'll miss it, you know,' said Lawrence.

'I'd miss a broken leg as well, but I wouldn't be sorry to see it go.' Even Val herself felt that this was somewhat harsh and a bit of an exaggeration. She'd loved her time as President and wouldn't have foregone a single minute. Still, she knew she was right in this instance – it was time to step down.

***

When Lally arrived next morning, her first words were 'Did you know your gnome's all smashed up, Mrs Khan?'

Ah well. She'd done her best. Time now to leave her future to fate.

JUNE

GILBERT AND SULLIVAN
or
The Undoing Of The Mature Woman.

Mrs Khan was deep in thought. Her photo albums, some not opened for the best part of fifty years, were on the table in front of her. The evening sun was starting to fail and whilst it wasn't cold, she could feel the temperature dropping slightly as the day closed in.

***

Mrs Khan had rarely been moved to speak at a W.I. meeting but today was totally unprecedented.

'Mr Bennet, I take your point regarding operas of Gilbert and Sullivan. I must be totally honest with you and admit I know none of them. But it seems to me from what you have shared with us this afternoon in your excellent talk that it is not undoing of mature woman that is at stake here but undoing of silly people round them disregarding their wisdom and beauty and finding them figures of fun. The songs you played for us show rounded but sad and lonely people. Not lonely because of personal defect but because surrounded by morons. Please forgive if I speak out of turn.' She sat down to a round of applause.

***

Over another exceptional pot of tea, this one being the 'definitive blend' created by her and Lally to be sold at the Summer Fair as 'Stackton-on-Sea W.I. Special', she was contemplating the contents of the albums lying there waiting to reveal long forgotten jewels.

Choosing the most recent first, she opened it to see a photograph of herself and Mr Khan with Gos and Amir, their wives and four small grandchildren here in this very garden several summers ago, the last one taken of Mr Khan before his untimely departure twelve years earlier.

She made her way through the albums slowly, until the light became too poor for her to see them clearly. Picking up the two oldest, she made her way into the lounge to continue her journey along the tracks of passed time.

**

'You make a very good point well put, Mrs Khan. Gilbert's treatment of the women in the texts he wrote was sympathetic, as was the music Sullivan set the words to. Their songs are some of the most beautiful in the G and S canon. However, the response of the other characters in the stories suggests an affirmation of a negative attitude to women of mature years – ' '*could somebody please translate that last sentence?' thought Kathy.* ' – and could be said to be both accepting and encouraging of the way in which the older woman is often perceived, sadly even today.'

'From what you've said in your talk,' said Val, 'I think we all feel that you don't like the pictures painted in these operas. It strikes me that the fact the women involved always ended up with the most prominent if not necessarily the most sought after, and, I have to say, usually much younger men suggests that they have the last laugh. Would you agree with that?'

'I very much hope that that is the case. We never discover how the matches pan out, as the shows always end at the point of union. With any luck, these somewhat shallow young men will find the sagacity of their spouses will rub off on them and be life enhancing.'

'More long words,' thought Kathy. 'Still, he's made a few interesting points this afternoon. It'll be interesting writing this one up for the Stackton Quarterly.'

***

This envelope had never been opened. Her sister had sent it when she received news of Mrs Khan's whereabouts. It was the last contact they'd ever had.

'What do you think, Harish?' she asked, surprised at the sound of own her voice registering in her ears. She was even surprised more to hear 'Do it, Mina. Do it with my love and blessing.'

***

'I found your talk extremely interesting, Mr Bennet' ventured Bryony –

'Bob, please'

'If I must. Rob,' she said, unswayed by his charm. 'I'm also quite pleased that someone has brought attention to the underlying misogyny in these so-called works of art, the moreso because it's a man who's done the deed and acknowledged, too, that the representation of young women is no longer relevant either. What you haven't told us is precisely how you personally feel about all this. I recognise that our President has taken it upon herself to speak for us and assume that you are against the vilification of the older woman and you have intimated that might be the case' – *good for you, Bryony, thought Kathy. Make as long a speech as you can spin out and use as many long words as you can think of* – 'you have not stated that unequivocally.' There was a certain hectoring arrogance in the way this was delivered and the women (with the exception of Kathy, who thought he was getting his just desserts) felt rather uncomfortable. Bob, however, didn't seem to notice anything at all amiss. Maybe he'd heard it all before.

'I think they were writing in the spirit of the time. I don't approve of it but I wasn't around at the time to tell them so.' (*Polite laughter from the floor.* 'I think that modern productions do their best to redress the balance but there's always more that can be done, not least of all with people like me – and your good self, I hope' – (*snort from Bryony*) – 'spreading awareness of the fundamental error in extant thinking when these works were written and sadly, still shared by too many people.' This answer seemed to satisfy even her.

The refreshment break had been an odd affair that afternoon. There was the usual sociable babble, naturally. The cakes and biscuits were as popular as ever and Mrs Khan had done her best to keep everyone's cup filled. The Summer Fair would be upon them very soon and the list Valerie had announced to them during her notices was on the board in the hut, waiting to be completed by eager volunteers. It didn't remain empty long. Most of the preparations were already in place but there were always things that couldn't be done until very close to the date.

The Fair was going to be a much bigger event this year. Any number of small groups had been getting together to make things and several of the shops in the town had asked to have stalls. The branch was already known in the County for the quality and quantity of merchandise on offer and now that there had been a couple of entertainments mounted, both universally accepted as being high quality and well worth the visit, their reputation had grown even stronger.

Valerie and Gina were off in a couple of days, their first foreign trip with the Brasso Choir, so Kathy was going to be holding the fort while they were away. It wouldn't be long. They were going to be away for a total of six days, so hopefully there'd be no major hiccups in that time. Val, though, was pretty sure that even if there were, Kathy would be well able to deal with them.

What was generating the odd feel to this month's social hour was the fact that they'd all been noddingly familiar with the music he'd been talking about and had taken it for granted for as long as they could remember, only it had been given a totally different and unexpected slant. Bob Bennet had certainly been an absorbing speaker and the extracts he'd brought with him were a pleasure to hear, but they'd never thought in those terms before. Gilbert and Sullivan, the archetypal creators of comic opera having all those political references and jokes at the heart of their writing. Now that really had been a revelation.

***

In her hand, Mrs Khan was holding a faded black and white print. On it were two girls playing by a natural pool. It must have been her brother who took the picture, as neither parent had cared much for cameras. She remembered that outfit so clearly, too young to be sari-clad and far too boisterous to have been able to keep one in place. She remembered the never-ending green foliage, disappearing into a distance far too great for such a young child to comprehend. She remembered also the three of them going off to look for lizards and Romesh teaching them how to recognise different bird songs.

If she was going to look at any more of these pictures, she needed to fortify herself with another pot of tea.

***

At the end of the afternoon, Bob was thanked and the women restored order to the hut, but they were more thoughtful than usual. These meetings were always interesting, often great fun and sometimes, like this one, unexpectedly provocative.

Once the hut was tidy and the door locked, Valerie started her walk back home. It was such a beautiful evening. She wondered if Lawrence fancied an evening out. She was just in the mood.

***

After much searching, Mrs Khan had found what she was looking for online. She logged into the Facebook account Gos had opened for her and got the page up she needed.

Dear Gita, she typed. This is your sister, Mina.

She pressed 'send' and put the computer away, afterwards making her way – very late – for a good night's rest.

WE'RE GOING ON A NESSIE HUNT...

Beth had never told anyone why she was so keen to find Nessie. The women asked lots of times and tried to discover what she was hoping to find. 'I want to go alone and I want to see Nessie with my own eyes,' was all she'd ever say. Because I'm telling the story, I really should know the answer. Unfortunately, she never let me into her secret either.

They were right about this, though. Sitting on the bank of the loch, the midges were definitely eating her alive and it was only June. It got much worse later so she was told and for that reason alone was quite pleased she hadn't waited.

'Enjoying the view?' The sound of a human voice made her jump. Apart from ordering food and buying knick-knacks, she'd not said a word to another soul since she got here.

'Very much.' She replied.

'Your first time?' he asked.

'Yes. Well, no, I came here when I was young but it's all lost from memory now.' She hoped her nose hadn't grown. 'How about you? I'm guessing from your accent you're local. Is this a regular haunt?'

'I live over there.' He indicated a small group of houses close to the loch. 'All this is visible from my home. I can see why it appeals to you.'

'Ever seen Nessie?' she asked.

He laughed. 'On a daily basis. It takes a trained eye, though. She's a very secretive creature.' Beth couldn't be absolutely sure he was pulling her leg.

'Ah, do you think she reveals herself only to those who believe?'

'Of course. Isn't that the way with all mythical beasties?' he asked with a twinkle in his eye. Emboldened, Beth enquired 'And are you willing to share the secret with me?'

***

Whilst Gloria had proved herself to be woefully incapable when it came to the preparation of chocolate treats, she'd proved herself exceptionally good at the production of beautiful, eye-catching designs for the boxes, wrappers and what little advertising Dorothy (and the WI) would permit. She'd had a few proofs printed for the new batch and took them round to Dorothy to see how she felt about using them for the Fair produce.

'They're beautiful,' said Dorothy. 'If you'd be interested in all that side of things for good, it'd leave me free to get on with the chocolatiering.'

'Sounds like a good division of labour to me,' said Gloria and went back home with new lightness to her gait and heart. It was working out after all.

***

The experience that surprised Beth most was the museum. They'd presented all the necessary evidence to prove there was no such creature but once you'd been round the exhibits – the diving bell! Fancy going down in that!

– watched the film and came out the other side, there was a truly mahoosive shop selling every manner of memorabilia created in the known universe and lots that could only be envisioned by someone with an extremely fertile and creative brain. She'd decided to take back a dozen green, smiling Nessies, one for the Bucket List cabinet in the W.I. hut, one for Mrs Khan and the others for various friends and family members. This had been a good idea.

'I'm staying over there in that big hotel.' It was very swish and within walking distance of the bank, costing her the equivalent of housekeeping for at least two months but this was such a special holiday, there was no point in being a cheapskate.

'Have you made lots of new friends?' he enquired.

'No, I've not really spoken to anyone much. There's been so little time.'

'What have you been up to?' he wanted to know.

'Well, an excursion to Inverness and then a day out in *or should it be on? she thought* 'the Black Isle. We went to a small village and stumbled across a harp maker,' said Beth.

'Do you play?' he asked.

'No, but I have a couple of good friends who do.'

***

Back in the W.I. hut, Kathy was getting a little overwhelmed by the sheer volume of goods being brought in by the women. Mrs Khan was on refreshment duties again.

'Would you like help with checking in, Mrs Borthwick?' she offered.

'Oh please, Mrs K. I don't know which way to turn with all this. The hall and I are being buried alive!'

In spite of the comprehensive list of instructions, it was going to be complicated and take a lot more that the two allocated hours.

'Come back Valerie!' pleaded Kathy under her breath, 'only not until I can prove that I didn't let the place fall into the bowels of hell in your absence!'

Apart from anything else the diorama Di Lewis had made was exquisite and was going to need careful storage. How did she do it? It was a perfect representation of a meeting in the Hut. Even the members were recognisable. It must have taken her months. Obviously, it would have to be a permanent fixture not a sale item, but still, what a lovely thought to have its first showing at the Summer Fair. 'I wish I could get to know her a bit better,' thought Kathy. But it wasn't her choice to make, so she left Di to her own devices.

With the stock they already had, Val's preparation had been meticulous but even she couldn't have foreseen all this. Kathy had only to tick things off as she checked through the cupboards and make a catalogue of anything that arrived today but that 'only', she decided, hid a virtual megaton of pitfalls. Helena was going to sort the stage out for her show and Kathy, not being what she called a 'theatre type' was more than happy to leave her to it.

**

Getting ready to go and collect Chelsea, Lally hoped she wasn't falling in love. She was missing Gos far more than she'd bargained for. They'd propped each other up and his return to the US to finalise his relocation had opened up a void in her spirit as well as her schedule. There'd been none of the – well, we all know what we're talking about here, so I'm not going to spell it out. But still, she'd enjoyed his company and found their heart-to-hearts both comforting and nourishing. She'd popped back to get some odds and ends left behind in a cupboard, not having realised earlier that she might need them.

As Gos was away, hearing the key in the lock startled her, but nowhere near as much as seeing Del walk into the living room, tanned, toned muscles, designer clothing and a haircut that must have come straight from one of the top men's hairstylists in Bristol. Feeling shabby, she reminded herself that her own wardrobe was perfectly fine for the life she lived and wearing recycled clothes helped the planet and the charities who supplied it. Still, she couldn't hold back the pang of longing for a new dress and a pair of posh shoes. Stunned into silence, she stared at him, unsure of what sort of reaction might be suitable in someone encountering a spouse who'd not come home from work nearly a year ago and had maintained radio silence ever since.

'We can put all this behind us babes. Let's start again.'

Lally was unable to speak. She knew she had to get out to pick Chelsea up, if nothing else, and if she stayed here she couldn't be sure what she might do. She had to find a way to move her legs and walk past him but her feet felt like they were buried beneath the floor tiles. How could he just walk back in, like nothing had happened and inform her he was here to stay?

'Say something, babes.' He said. 'Don't just gawp at me like I'm a goldfish breathing out fire.'

'Hell,' thought Lally. 'What do I do? What can I say? Why can't I speak?' Maybe best not to, she decided, given that she had no idea what the right words would be. She'd almost forgotten him in the whirlwind of keeping her life going and seeing that Chelsea didn't suffer. They'd managed without him and it'd been okay. Not great, but okay, and she'd rubbed along just fine. Even Chelsea didn't seem to miss him much anymore.

'I need to pick up Chelsea,' she managed eventually.

'Great,' he said. 'I'll come with you.'

'No, you won't. Be somewhere else when I get back. I don't want you in my life anymore.'

Now, neither of them had been expecting that.

***

'Are you sure this is a genuine Scottish wine?' asked Beth.

'Most definitely. Why are you so surprised?'

'It's just that I never thought of Scotland as being a wine producing region,' she replied.

She'd never have chosen this restaurant, gravitating towards the cheap-and-cheerful end of the market herself. But it was excellent food and, she had to admit, outstanding wine and the company was even better for being totally unexpected. Max knew how to treat a woman, for sure and whilst she was firmly married, what the hell? It was only an evening out and another one of those once-in-a-lifetime events that were becoming rather commonplace in the annals of the Stackton-on-Sea WI. Tomorrow she was going to see if someone could tell her where to find the chap who devoted his whole life to Nessie hunting, living in a shack on the shore. But tonight, well, tonight could go on forever.

***

Lally sat on the bench where she'd first encountered Gos. She wasn't silly enough to think or hope that things might have been different. No point in dreaming of the land-that-might-have-been and he had his own demons to cast out. She wondered how he and Ren were getting on. Well, she hoped they weren't really getting on at all. In fact, she hoped much more fervently than she should have done if he were simply the friend she'd thought he was. Was it because of him she found she had no interest in Del? She'd been happy with him before he'd abandoned the two of them but that was then. This was now. She'd changed, and he must have done, too. The question was, did she want to get to know the new Del and was she willing to let him discover the new Lally? Wearily, she got up from the bench and made her way to Dorothy's, where she suspected Chelsea would have been eating much more chocolate than she'd been making, having missed out on the last opportunity. At least that part of life was predictably normal.

***

'I've never seen her but I know she's out there.' The two of them were sitting in a surprisingly comfortable shack drinking extremely refreshing tea, brewed on an old camping stove. Beth marvelled at what it must take to be so committed to something that it was worth giving up everything to live like this.

'How can you be so sure?' asked Beth.

'How can we ever be sure of anything?'

Fair point, she thought. The sound of the waves reminded her of Stackton. What a lot she'd have to talk about at their Bucket List evening in November.

***

'When's Gos coming back, mummy?' asked Chelsea.

'Not for a while, pet. And when he does, he'll probably have his wife with him, so it won't be quite the same as it was before.'

'Couldn't you be his wife?'

'No, sweetheart. He can't have two. Do you think much about Daddy? You don't say much about him.'

'Daddy went away to be with someone else.' This was news to Lally.

'What makes you think that, darling?' she asked.

'We saw them sometimes when we were out.'

'Did he ever talk to you?'

'No. I used to hide. Why can't Gos leave his wife behind and move in with us?' she wanted to know. Lally found herself – reluctantly – thinking the same thing.

***

'You will keep in touch, won't you?' asked Max.

'You have my contact details, too, so you're just as capable.' Beth realised that sounded a lot more confrontational than she'd intended. 'What I meant is, you don't have to wait for me to pick up the phone. I'm happy to be receive calls, just as much as make them. Besides, there's always Zoom and Facebook, if that's easier.' Stop digging Beth, she told herself. She knew she was taking a chance, but well, what were the chances he'd ever try to get in touch? A bit of flirting was fun and that's all it was. However wonderful this interlude had been, it was just that, an interlude, and she was about to make her way back to real life. As she was confident he'd never use it, giving him her phone number presented no problems at all, but it did make her feel good, being attractive to this delightful man. She knew perfectly well – or at least, suspected – that he picked up a different woman every time the previous one checked out of the hotel. 'When was the last time anyone gave you a second look? Made you feel attractive?' she asked herself but could come up with no answer.

The journey to the airport seemed to be much quicker than it had on the day of her arrival. And yes, Mrs Khan had been right (again) – far better not to find non-existent monsters than to find non-existent monsters; and in any case, that particular monster had turned out to be a beloved pet.

BARCELONA

'Valerie, my love. As much as I adore you and as wonderful an addition as you've been to my life, there are times when you talk total tosh and this is one of them.'

Val saw herself as a calm, level headed sort of woman. This, though, was challenging that image.

'Honestly, Lawrence, I don't think I should go. I'm not a singer, not really, and it's going to be a big concert in a strange place.'

'You've sung this programme twice already with about a hundred and twenty other people, in front of a paying audience, once in the Cathedral and once in a concert hall, both times with an orchestra. Stop being silly.'

'It's alright for you, Lawrence. You've been doing this since you were a teenager. It's part of your daily life.'

'I was born neither playing the harp nor sitting in an orchestra pit. We only become comfortable with anything at all by doing it.'

She'd been tempted to ask him to go with them but Gina's husband was adamant that she should stay at home. So, she thought, it would be insensitive to leave Gina to share a hotel room with a stranger. Gina believed Gil's objections stemmed from the fact that he didn't want to have to cook his own meals for a few days but he claimed it was because he was worrying about her book keeping business.

'Look Gil,' she told him 'I've had this business for more than twenty five years, since long before you and I had even met. I know how to organise my time so the business won't suffer.' But he refused to be convinced. He'd been wandering around with a face like a pickled sardine ever since she told him she'd been selected. Of course, he had to keep reminding her that she'd been a reserve and only chosen because one of the teachers hadn't been able to get leave. He'd refused to go to any of their concerts and kept telling her she was making a fool of herself. She was extremely surprised. Normally he supported everything she did. But, she thought cynically, until this, all I've ever done is go to W.I. meetings and earn money.

**

'Music, concert dress, make up, cool clothes, Euros – is there anything on the list I've not put in?'

'A bit of Stackton-on-Sea W.I. spirit might come in handy,' replied Lawrence.

Valerie was being forced to admit with alarming regularity that Lawrence made a lot of sense. Not that she didn't but it was a very different sense from hers. Being her first (and, she hoped, only) marriage, entered upon in later years, she was unfamiliar with the humdrum challenges faced by cohabiting couples every day. In general, the learning process was rather fun.

They picked up Gina and drove off to the airport, bumping into several other choir members in the departure lounge. For their colleagues, it was nothing new but to Val and Gina, this was the equivalent of a solo round the world boat trip. They both hoped they wouldn't capsize and drown.

**

Their first concert left them on an astronomical high, buzzing and tingling all over.

'Well ladies, how did you enjoy that?' They recognised the tall man from the rehearsals. He was addressing them rather superciliously and – thought Gina, rather presumptuously – but had never been introduced so they did the honours themselves.

'I'm Gina and this is Valerie, Lawrence's wife. You know, Lawrence Ford, the harpist.' She rather hoped that would put him in his place but didn't think there was much chance. 'This is our first concert abroad.'

He didn't bother to fill them in with his name, simply informed them that 'It's such a great shame. All that messy stuff at the beginning of the second half. And the tenor soloist! Really! Where do they get these people from?' He would have preferred it, so he said, had the "ladies" (*Who in the world uses that expression these days apart from some of the other W.I. members? Good job Bryony's not here to hear it, thought Gina*) had their first experience in a really good show, not the appalling mess this had been.

'Bugger off,' said Gina, causing Valerie to involuntarily raise her eyebrows. Not that she objected – her own feelings were a perfect match – but she'd never heard the usually pacific Gina so much as allow an edge onto her voice. 'We had a wonderful time and you're not going to spoil it for us. Come on Val.' So saying, she drew Valerie away and they spent a happy hour wandering along the pavement looking at the stalls with their jewellery, gifts and light clothing, popping in for a quick nightcap at one of the cafes and every so often bursting into song, much to the amusement of the crowd.

***

As we know, the W.I. year finishes in August and Dorothy realised she'd have to make a decision very soon. The trouble was, she'd made such a wonderful dossier on each of her three choices, so it was an absolute impossibility to make up her mind which was best. What to do?

***

Lawrence, sitting by the French windows leading out to the garden, was flattered to receive the call. It wasn't something he'd been accustomed to, being phoned by someone and asked for advice. He decided against tea and coffee, preferring to offer some of the excellent wine he'd accumulated over the years. After all, this was a special occasion, one that he hoped would be repeated often in the future.

After her second glass of Sauvignon Blanc, Dorothy started to loosen up a bit. It was new to her as well, asking for help like this. He'd given her the choice of a couple of reds, a white and a rose and she'd gone for this one. 'Maybe the odd glass isn't such a bad thing, after all,' she thought.

So, here they were, the erstwhile notoriously crabby and prickly Lawrence, and the shy, buttoned-up Dorothy, enjoying each other's company over an alcoholic beverage. Things change, we all know that, but Lawrence and Dorothy were pushing the boundaries to the absolute limit.

'You see,' she said,' there are pros and cons to all three places. I've thought so much I've sent myself down a blind alley.'

'Could that be a little too much vino a bit too quickly and on an empty stomach?' thought Lawrence, but kept it to himself, realising it wasn't a kind thought.

'And I figured, well, you've been all over the world playing your harp. You might be able to help me with my decision.'

Lawrence quickly decided against telling her that the inside of a concert hall was much the same whether in Birmingham or Tokyo. That would be a reversion to the old, pre-Valerie days, when he was, shall we say, a little less welcoming. Besides, he was enjoying this entirely unexpected meeting and didn't want to spoil it.

'Right, m'dear,' he said, instantly regretting the familiarity. It was okay though. Dorothy didn't appear to have noticed. He just hoped she wasn't a bit too tipsy. What had he done, suggesting wine to this sweet woman? In his defence, she hadn't told him she was 'normally tee-total' until halfway through the second glass – 'a particularly fine example,' he thought, brought back from the New Zealand tour a year or so ago – but still. He might have been a little more vigilant. 'The way it seems to me is that we should make a chart.'

Dorothy was on firm ground here. She knew all about charts, especially now there were at least three on the notice board of the W.I. hut. 'We have four columns: Country, Pros, Cons, and the last one with a score in it. Pros get a positive, cons get a negative and at the end of the process we tot them all up and you have your answer.'

'Why didn't I think of that?' wondered Dorothy in the privacy of her own head.

So, they spent the evening pondering on the relative merits of the three destinations chosen, with Dorothy being careful to resist the temptation to drink any more of the wine that Lawrence had ceased to offer her.

***

The Wizard was taking another look around Stackton. Although he'd not been as impressed at Christmas as he was last summer, he knew that things can get a bit out of hand round that time of year and figured it might have been a fluke. The theatre had an interesting mix of amateur shows put on by the many local dramatic societies and professional theatre companies touring their productions in the hope that they'd be taken up by one of the larger venues in the country's towns and cities. There were some music evenings, as well, covering quite a wide range of styles. His programme only went to the end of August and they'd told him the brochure covering September to December would be out soon. He'd be able to pick that up with no difficulty, as he was here until at least mid-August.

They were friendly enough and the theatre building itself was welcoming but the possibilities were vast and largely untapped. They needed someone like him, he was sure. He could get an architect to sort out a revamp, completely refit the place so that it looked like it belonged to the twenty first century, upgrade the café, which was pitifully ill equipped and serving very little to tempt the refined palette. The inaugural concert would have to be with local artistes, that went without saying. Those two harpists, for instance, and the actress who did the one-woman show – Helena Daly – she was good. And a crowd puller too. She'd need to get a few facial fillers and update her hairstyle but apart from that, she was pretty impressive. This was getting to be an exciting proposition.

He stopped off at a waterfront café and ordered himself fish and chips. No sense in coming to a seaside town in the UK without sampling the national dish, was there?

**

The Cocoa Bean Venture Chart was filling up nicely. Lawrence felt that Sri Lanka's elephants could well swing the whole thing in its favour, in spite of him reminding her that it probably wasn't all like the places they showed in that lovely TV programme on a Sunday evening in the winter and it was unlikely (although not impossible) that elephants roamed free anymore. Moreover, he didn't think they'd ever showed a cocoa bean plantation during the entire course of the series. 'How many are there over there now?' he asked. She wasn't sure but knew there were fewer than there had been. 'Maybe I should go there before they all close down,' she said. 'Okay,' he replied. 'How many points does that warrant in the pros list?' 'On the other hand,' she told him, 'there's a lot of unrest over there.' 'Okay,' he said. 'How many points do you want to knock off for that?'

This was a great deal more complicated than either of them had foreseen.

**

Back in Barcelona, the next day was free, so sight-seeing in Barcelona was a given. They were both very tired and had a good long lie in, meaning they missed breakfast at the hotel.

Barcelona had been on Val's personal bucket list well before the W.I. created their own, so this was super – special for her. In the few times she wasn't drunk on the joy of making music, she was drunk on the sights and sounds of her dream city, even bumping into a harpist busking outside a restaurant in a side street. Gina, who was as over-whelmed by it all as Val was, sunk herself into the moment and switched off her thinking self altogether.

Their final concert was both exhilarating and sad. This evening meant it was all coming to an end and real life would start again in less than twenty four hours. They made the most of the post-concert reception – avoiding the tall, dark but not especially handsome stranger from the first night – and enjoyed the company of all the new people they'd met on this all-too-short trip.

***

'So the thing about Trinidad and Tobago is that we meet lots of people from that part of the world here and it would be nice to know a little bit more about their heritage.'

'I suspect,' thought Lawrence, 'that most of the people we meet were born and bred here and have never been there either.'

'I mean, I know a lot of the young ones won't have been born or grown up there but when you're my age, you meet lots who were,' said Dorothy.

'I stand corrected,' thought Lawrence. 'Well then,' he said, 'let's start rating the pros and cons. How many for "want to see a bit of the country where lots of my friends/ acquaintances were born?"' He duly entered the figure in the right column. 'And how many in the cons column for "I can go there on holiday any time I like, like lots of my friends already do?"' That, too, was entered in the relevant grid box. They were starting to get somewhere.

***

The coach took them to the airport bright and early. They were each lost in their private thoughts on the journey home. Gina had a jumble of emotions coursing through her – excitement, delight, optimism, pleasure; but also concern and, it had to be admitted, a tiny amount of fear. What was the reception going to be when she got home? Gil had said he wouldn't meet her, so Lawrence was going to drop her off on the way back with Val. She silently rehearsed all the arguments they might have when she went through the door with her suitcase.

Val, on the other hand, suffered no such ambiguity of thinking or feeling. Lawrence had been right. Any fears she'd had were unfounded and she knew that this was something she wanted to do more of. Much, much more, in fact. And she so, so wanted to take an even more active part in Lawrence's musical life. It was becoming almost an obsession for her. There was the odd moment when she wondered if she were as much in love with the career he followed as the man himself. She knew there wasn't a lot in her armoury to offer but she could attend rehearsals, like he'd suggested to her – she'd always said no, feeling like an imposter – go on tour with him, spend more time with his – their, she hoped – friends from that world and not feel so silly about asking questions and expressing her pleasure. He'd said to her often enough, 'Valerie, my love, there's no right or wrong when it comes to our responses to music. It's how you feel that matters. It won't be the same as anyone else, but that doesn't make it invalid. It just makes it yours.' Yes, he'd definitely been right.

***

After dropping Dorothy home – couldn't let her walk home in that state, he thought – he'd pondered on the success of the evening. He rather liked being the facilitator in problem solving and thought seriously that he might drop by on Gil one evening and see if he could say something useful about Gina's entry into the world of singing. Now, if he could thaw Gil a bit, that really could be a success story.

Dorothy was excited as she got herself ready for bed. She'd had such a lovely time and they'd made the perfect decision. Guyana it was!

There'd be time enough in the morning to start finding plantations and looking into flights and accommodation. Tonight, all she wanted to do was tuck herself down and dream about the wonderful trip that she was going to make in the not-too-distant future.

'What a nice man that Lawrence is,' she thought as her head hit the pillow. 'I can see exactly why he won Valerie's heart and what a wonderful harp teacher he's been to Mrs. Khan.'

At least, that was what she tried to think. She was too quickly asleep to finish the thought. Dorothy's new dawn had broken.

***

Kathy was recovering nicely from the day's tribulations at the hut. It was so lovely that they all put such a lot into making these fund raising affairs a success but she wasn't quite as familiar with it all as Val, and in her heart, she didn't really want to be.

The talk they'd had on the estuary had been another good one and she'd ordered herself that book on identification of animals and plants Ruth had recommended. It'd be good to know what she was looking at when she went down there with Boris, her recently acquired west Highland terrier. Mrs Khan had bought the book herself and found it really useful. Kathy's entry on this year's Bucket List to learn Spanish had fallen by the wayside. It'd turned out to be a great deal more difficult than she'd expected, what with there being no-one to practice with. Kathy had

had several entries since they'd started making these lists, the first two having been to take a roller-coaster ride – which she'd done with Mrs Khan – and to get a rescue dog, the aforementioned Boris. He'd made a big difference to her everyday living. He didn't need much walking, so didn't impact badly on her 'manky bones and joints' as she described them, although she had noticed that she was going a bit further and a bit faster these days. Her husband had made it clear that the dog was her responsibility and showed no signs of changing that standpoint.

She wondered how Valerie and Gina were enjoying their time away. Maybe she'd call round to Lawrence to see how he was getting on and if he'd heard anything. They'd not really known him before he got married but he seemed a lot more approachable now or possibly he'd just been a bit shy and standoffish in the presence of all those women. She hoped that was the case, although if it wasn't, it could possibly be evidence that the presence a good woman could, after all, turn a frog into a prince. 'And I'm Bradley Walsh in drag', she told herself, clearly not being taken in by her own optimism.

***

'I've missed you so much, darling,' Gil had put his arms round Gina and kissed her warmly on the neck. This was the one response she hadn't prepared for. 'Can I come with you next time?'

The four of them exchanged greetings and Gina, taken aback by the open-hearted welcome she'd received, suggested they all go for coffee before they left the airport. The general feeling was no, it was best to get back. Gina's second surprise was that Gil had brought his own car.

'What now?' she thought. 'Am I going to be told we're going bankrupt, all because I went away for a few days?' But no. It was because Gil wanted to share some time with her and find out what it'd been like for her being away to sing. 'How long can this last?' she asked herself before deciding that it didn't matter. She'd enjoy it while it did.

On their own drive back home, Valerie was thoughtful. She had no idea at all of what had been going on while she was away, with either Dorothy or Gil. 'That was quite a turnaround from Gina's husband, wasn't it?'

'Mm,' answered Lawrence, keeping his eyes firmly on the road.

'I wonder what made him change his stand so dramatically,' she said, trying to get a glimpse of him from the corner of her eye.

Lawrence, following the example of Captain Pugwash's inestimable cabin boy, the wise and wonderful Tom, simply smiled and said nothing.

HARISH

Taking Chelsea out today was a godsend. Mrs Khan wanted, no, *needed* a distraction. As much as she'd loved having Gos there, his return to the USA at the end of May had come at a good time. In any case, he said he thought he might be coming back with Ren at the end of July, so they could look for a family home, renting at first to check that they'd be happy to make such a dramatic move. Mrs Khan was not so sure, but kept her silence.

Now that she was going to school for odd 'practice days', little Chelsea was an even more live wire than ever. Most of the time, if she wasn't at nursery Lally took her to appointments with her but today she was seeing Del for an adult conversation regarding the future. 'About time he did something to sort himself out' thought Mrs Khan but, in her usual way, would never have dreamed of being rude enough to say so. Chelsea had requested another visit to the duck pond and this was one of Mrs Khan's favourite outings as well, so she was only too happy to oblige.

Once the ducks had had their fill – 'if such a thing is possible,' thought Mrs Khan. 'They seem to be able to go on eating for ever' – the two of them went to the ice cream parlour, Mrs Khan enjoying a coconut sorbet and Chelsea tucking into a Knickerbocker glory almost as big as she was herself.

She wondered if Gos really believed her daughter-in-law might be willing to take a turn at British life. She'd never lived anywhere other than America and England was so different. His new position started in September and Mrs K hoped that they'd have their house sorted out by then – 'cutting it fine,' she thought – if, indeed, it was going to be the two of them together. Ren worked in the beauty industry for a big international and would undoubtedly hope to continue with the same job in Bristol. Charlene, Amir's wife, was a doctor and thought Ren to be some-what shallow, whereas Ren found Charlene too serious. However, the two women rubbed along okay when the occasion arose. Fortunately for all concerned, such times were rare. In her heart, Mrs K really didn't think there was much chance of Ren relocating and couldn't believe Gos thought so either, or even that he honestly wanted her to.

***

Almost caressing the envelope, Mrs Khan was having second thoughts about opening this last remnant of a life forever left behind. Tigger had jumped up onto her lap and snuggled in to her body, like he knew she might need a bit of comfort. 'More like he thinks that way he'll get extra treats' she thought, remembering again the talk they'd had on cat behaviour at the beginning of the current W.I. season. Then, 'Buck up,' she said out loud, hoping that the neighbours weren't in the garden. 'Are you going to do this or not?' So saying, she ran her finger along the crease and took the one remaining photograph from its covering.

She was looking at her seventeen year old self, smiling happily at the camera, Harish with his arm round her looking as happy as any man ever could. Her parents hadn't approved. Their girl could do better than someone who'd come to work on the plantation to pick tea, but then, (she thought now) what parent doesn't want the best they can find for their daughter? For their sons, also, she added, being a mother of two herself.

It was the last photo taken of her before she and Harish ran away to who knows what, so they could build a life together whether her parents liked it or not. She'd never seen any of her family again, nor her home nor, indeed, her country – Ceylon, as it was back then – and had never regretted the decision she'd made.

It was a long evening that Mrs Khan sat holding the photograph, letting her mind wander wherever it wanted to take her. Then: 'Enough,' she told herself. 'You had life you chose and it was wonderful. No room for regrets in this heart.'

She fed Tigger and didn't bother to look at her emails that night. Whatever there was in them could wait.

JULY

THE STACKTON-ON-SEA W.I.
'RUN FOR CHARITY' SPORTS DAY

Well, here it was at last. The Sports Day. Well, Sports Morning, really. There'd been no shortage of volunteers and from what they could tell, there'd be no shortage of competitors, either.

Di Lewis, (the constable's wife) won the Egg and Spoon race. No-one was sure if it was because she was truly best at balancing an egg on a piece of cutlery or that the other women wanted to make up for her lost time and let her win. After all, this was her entry on the grid.

It was the first event of the day, so there weren't that many observers yet, which probably helped. Di chose not to take a prize but was proud of her medal. She was taking part in everything, whether or not she had any hope of winning, and let's be honest, even she knew there was little chance of that if athletic talent was the sole criterion on which success was to be based. Chelsea had made a set of medals out of cardboard and ribbon for the first three in every event and Lally had painstakingly marked them all up with event and position.

Di had done all the organising, right from getting permission for the use of the Green to setting up the tables for donations and entry fees, although the other women had helped when necessary. There were twenty three entries from W.I. members and so far, twelve from non-members. They were only charging two pounds a go so it hadn't raised a fortune yet for the *Let's Share Allotment* but there were bound to be more during the day and there was a donation box. There was no refreshments table – the women didn't want to take business away from the local cafes and restaurants but there was a sales table, and the women had been generous with their contributions, both for selling and as prizes.

Choosing the events had been a bit more difficult than had been anticipated. After considerable deliberation, the Sports Day Committee decided against a three-legged race.

'It's all right for the young ones but for some of us, running with both our legs is difficult enough.'

'That's right. We don't want to go home with broken bones.'

There was a debate as to whether or not there should be an age or fitness limit.

'That'd be discriminatory.'

'But it makes sense. We've already said we don't want any fractures.'

'We're all adults. If we can't manage, we'll exclude ourselves. We're not going to take any chances.'

'There'll always be someone who overestimates what they can do, either from genuine lack of awareness or wishful thinking.' And so it went on. The debate took a lot longer than had been bargained for but in the end, the three-legged race was duly dropped, as, too, was the sack race. They agreed that men should be allowed to take part but would have races of their own. They just hoped it wouldn't rain.

***

Helena had decided she should get her feet back on the ground, what with living in the world of fantasy that sprung from a life in the theatre, even one in its infancy like hers, maybe even the moreso for being a novel pursuit. She'd been wondering what it was about baking that was getting everyone's creative juices coursing through their veins. She'd never seen the point herself. In Helena's estimation, the supermarket sold perfectly good cakes for most everyday needs and if there was a requirement for anything special, one of the W.I. women would always be happy to knock up something uniquely tasty in a the blink of an eye for a tiny fraction of what it would cost from a commercial baker. Still, even Val had started to make her own since she'd decided to take a hike down the road of wedded bliss, so in an effort to bring herself back to terra firma, Helena phoned Mrs Khan and asked if she had a recipe for Victoria Sponge.

'Sorry, Miss Bailey. Not my type of cooking. Why not try internet? Most things are available from that source, I understand.'

She discovered she had most of the ingredients – eggs, sugar and butter – but no flour and nothing to bake in. A quick trip to Bestbuys remedied that and she returned home determined to make a cake to be proud of, maybe even a forerunner for one that she could put into future fairs for the WI. After all, cake is part of the staple diet in Stackton-on-Sea.

When she got it out of the oven, it looked truly amazing, even if it did dip a bit in the centre.

'Right. They say the proof of the pudding is in the eating,' she said out loud, and cut into it with not inconsiderable pride.

'Uurgh, oh my lord, yuck,' she spluttered, before spitting the offending mouthful into a paper handkerchief and throwing it down the toilet. She examined everything very carefully to ascertain where the mistake had occurred. On scrutiny of the bag of sugar, she discovered it was a calorie free substitute and she'd used twice as much as the recipe required. So, another trip to Bestbuys was in order to acquire the real thing.

***

Di's Bucket List wish to take part in a Sports Day had been born of having always been left out at school. She had two left feet and a nasty habit of bumping into things and people, sending them flying and causing danger to life, limb and property, even on one occasion, genuine injury, in the form of a broken wrist, not hers, but that of an unfortunate bystander who simply couldn't get out of the way in time. She was definitely going to make the most of this, even though she was feeling a bit queasy with nerves.

Mrs Khan was manning the sales table. She had no wish to take part in competitive sport, no matter how much fun it was supposed to be. 'That particular madness has not yet assailed me,' she thought. Sue was taking the money for entries and co-ordinating the races. Wellie Wanging looked like it was going to be extremely popular.

***

Back in her kitchen, Helena was in the throes of her next attempt – this one was going to be beyond perfect – to make a Victoria sponge to rival any of its kind in the known world, light, fluffy and melting on the tongue. While it was cooking, she realised she'd run out of raspberry jam with her first attempt, so popped down to Bestbuys to get some more. There'd just be time to get there and back before needing to remove the cake from the oven.

In the event, there was a long queue for the checkout – it was, after all, the height of the summer season – and by the time she got back, smoke was billowing from her kitchen such that she was half choked through having to breathe it in.

She opened the windows, closed the kitchen door and gave the flat time to recover before getting ready for attempt number three.

***

The day had gone well in every respect and Di had collected a good number of medals. The local paper had been down again to take photos and write a brief report, the Stackton W.I. now being a celebrity in its own right. They packed up that afternoon tired but happy, another satisfied member having acquired her tick on the Bucket List and a significant contribution having been collected for the *Let's Share Allotment*.

***

While the third Victoria Sponge was baking, Helena hunkered down to have a look at a play script she'd found in a charity shop. It was pleasant enough, one of those efforts that at one time would have been described as 'well crafted'. She got herself up and went to the kitchen to get a glass of water. As she was about to return, she noticed the eggs were still on the work surface.

'Oh well,' she thought. 'Some of us simply aren't cut out to be domestic goddesses,' and with that in mind, she chucked the whole lot in the bin and took an enormous slice of the fruit cake that she'd bought from the bakery on the seafront.

'Far tastier and infinitely less effort,' she said, and settled herself down to a satisfying evening of play reading.

***

Hanging on Di's reminder board, the stash of medals was impressive. If that wasn't enough cause for celebration, the GP had confirmed that she'd have to tell her boss she'd be taking maternity leave – the second thing in one day she never thought would happen, not after what happened last time. She was a bit nervous, but then, she'd have the time to get used to the idea over the course of the next eight-ish months or so; and they'd promised her she'd be monitored and monitored until she knew and understood the process far better than any of them did and was thoroughly bored with the whole process. 'Nothing will be left to chance, Mrs Lewis. You'll be in good hands,' he'd said and she'd believed him. Waiting for Jason to come home was torture. She'd ordered fish and chips and he was going to pick them up on the way back from his shift.

He was beaming as he came through the door. 'I got my promotion, Di,' he informed her practically dancing round the kitchen. 'And I had a positive pregnancy test,' was her reply. It was an evening that household would never forget.

CANAL HOPPING

Okay. We're talking July in England and we all know what that means. Exactly. Rain. And then a bit more rain. And then it stops to recharge its batteries and starts throwing it down again, this time more heavily and with a gusto impossible to envisage unless you've been in the Caribbean during the rainy season.

Not that Dr Di cared one bit. As far as narrowboats go, Andrew's was pretty luxurious and he was an excellent cook, an experienced and competent skipper and above all, fun. He'd owned it for the best part of thirty years and spent all his spare time on it, including long vacations in the summer, when he'd take whatever he needed and work in the cabin.

Dr Di wondered if they'd ever have got together had it not been for dinner with Val and Lawrence and concluded that no, they wouldn't. She'd shown plenty of interest in his talk on *The Bard's Naughty Bits* but he'd not indicated he wanted any further contact. For that matter, at that point neither had she. She felt quite chuffed that they'd manage to keep it all under wraps, although there'd been the odd difficult moment. She'd be less protective of their secret now that she felt more secure in the relationship.

So, as well as yet another Bucket List dream come true for the WI, Dr Di was enjoying wonderful company, tasty home-cooked Caribbean cuisine (as well as the odd takeaway and pub meal along the route), the pleasure of pootling along at four miles an hour instead of the usual frenetic life of a seaside GP and lots of – well, let's leave them to it.

***

Helena, on the other hand, was experiencing something different altogether.

'Fillers? Fillers? Really? What do you think I am? A crumbling molar needing to be fixed?' The Wizard was feeling mystified by this little outburst, as she was a tin-cy-wincy bit too mature for it to be related to the usual problem that women experience during their adult years, but she must surely realise that a little bit of help in the facial area could only help her. It was fortunate for him that he didn't expand on these opinions.

'I suggest you take your ideas for the Stackton Theatre and how to improve all our lives right back to wherever it is you hatched them up and use them to plug the cracks in your own face. Or maybe you already have thoughts on how to fill them. Skip-loads of slurry, perhaps? Bog off, Big Ears! And the name's Bailey, not Daly, you dick'ead!' She flounced out, leaving such a heavy grey mist behind her, The Wizard couldn't even see her go.

***

'That's a speckled wood,' said Andrew. 'We don't normally see butterflies along this part of the canal.'

'Can you identify all the fish and water birds as well?' she asked.

'Fish are more difficult, obviously, because they're not always that clear to see but mostly, yes.'

Dr Di was making the most of a short interlude of sunshine. The forecast had suggested it wouldn't last long. It was nice not to have to wear waterproofs on deck for a bit. 'Could you teach me how to handle the boat?' she asked. 'Sure,' he answered. 'It's not difficult. A bit awkward at times but nothing you won't be proficient at by the time the holiday's over.'

This was proving to be everything she'd ever hoped for and given the easy-going familiarity they were enjoying, in many ways it was even more.

***

'That was wonderful, Helena,' said Beth. 'You should start your own company and make it into a career.'

What do they think I'm trying to do? She thought. Helena still felt bruised by her earlier encounter and wasn't feeling inclined towards kindness.

The Summer Show had taken place a couple of evenings before the Fair, and Andrew had shot off to pick up Dr Di immediately the curtain came down, leaving Helena to deal with their adoring public.

'So creative and a stroke of genius to have Andrew playing the other parts!' These were just two of the accolades for her summer show. It was a relief. She wasn't able to gauge her own responses accurately at the moment. This was the second time she and Andrew had performed a two-hander written by her, and they were turning into quite an impressive double act, even though Andrew was an academic rather than an actor. He had natural talent, clearly, and wasn't shy of using it.

'It wasn't as easy to write as I'd bargained,' she admitted, 'even though all the lines were already there.' Andrew hadn't had any difficulty learning them. Indeed, he knew them all well before they started to rehearse but as he said, they weren't necessarily in the order he was used to. She'd used a mixture of Shakespeare and Noel Coward for this one. Much to her own surprise, it had worked.

The show had again raised a significant amount of money for the allotment, the last but one fundraiser before the new charity started to benefit in September. And, of course, they'd have a new President now that Val was branching out.

'The circle of life,' thought Helena. She hadn't told anyone she'd been selected to audition for a regular five minute spot on the local magazine programme, highlighting the fortunes – or otherwise – of seniors, *Golden Oldies*. She knew she'd never get it but it was fantastic to have got this far. Fillers indeed! The man was a puffed up fool!

***

'Don't you just love these evenings, sitting out here with nothing but the sounds of the river and the dimming of the light?'

Given the almost unrelenting rain during their time away, they were maybe not the words she would have chosen herself, but this was their last evening and Dr Di was making the most of it. Tomorrow they'd be back and living on terra firma again. As luck would have it, their last full day had been bright and warm.

'You've never told me how you ended up living on the canal.'

'It happened by chance and imperceptibly really,' said Andrew. 'I was doing my postgraduate studies in

Birmingham and it was the cheapest way to live back then,' he said. 'I loved it and although I'd intended a more conventional life, it never really happened.' To Dr Di, it seemed as if he'd been born living on a narrowboat and couldn't imagine him in any other context. 'Even though I've got a proper house in Bristol now, this is where I choose to spend my time, as long as it's possible. How about you? What attracted you to the joys of the narrowboat? A love of canals? A need for a less conventional lifestyle away from the stress of a busy surgery and demanding patients?' They'd spent a few weekends and evenings on the boat, but this was their first real stretch of time together and the only time they'd taken the boat out. It was giving them the chance to see different sides of each other.

'All of the above, but it was something that appealed even before my student days.' His life had been so different from her own, which had followed a completely traditional route of school, medical school and general practice. 'There was never really the opportunity to do anything about it. It's not something I wanted to do alone and everyone I asked couldn't see the appeal of being trapped in a boat six feet wide moving slower than the average snail. The thing that clinched it for most of them was the lack of a television.'

Bursting into their relaxed and rather intimate exchange came 'Room for a little one?' Judy, one of what Di considered 'the true boat people', waited a split second before making her way on deck. She gave Andrew an enthusiastic but coy kiss on the cheek *how do you express both of those things at the same time? wondered Dr Di. Does it take years of practice?* and greeted Di with prayer hands.

After the introductions were made, they all sat down to another glass of vino. It wasn't quite how Dr Di had pictured their final evening. 'So how did you end up living on the canal?' she enquired, not really bothered one way or the other but she had to say something, and given that Di was feeling acutely that she was in the way, she either had to make the effort or go to bed. Alone.

'I was a nurse, didn't earn much, couldn't afford a house so thought that a houseboat would be my only chance of my own home.' Judy, too, felt that Di was in the way and was making a good deal less effort to conceal it.

'Why a static boat rather than a cruiser?' Make the questions short and sweet, she said to herself, don't encourage her to expand too much.

'Oh, that's easy. I can't tell my left from my right and found it too difficult to navigate.' '

How did you manage to nurse then? thought Di uncharitably and with no grounds for such a thought whatsoever. Oh please go! This is my last night on a boat, possibly forever! Let me enjoy it in peace!

At this point, Andrew stepped in. 'Okay, ladies. I know you have things you like to talk about that you can't say in front of men friends, so I'm going below deck to do some work.'

Two hearts sank. Two minds thought simultaneously 'Oh hell! What do I do now?'

After a few more forlorn attempts to make conversation, Di was pleased when Judy said thanks but it was time to go home. She called down to tell Andrew she was leaving, who replied but didn't bother to make an appearance, so she went back to her own home, feeling that she'd missed another rather more important boat.

'So, how does it feel to have had your first taste of the joys of narrowboating?' asked Andrew, pouring the last of the wine into their glasses.

'Great. Just great.' They'd be back home tomorrow morning but this evening, there was still plenty of time to pretend it would never come to an end.

'The first of many? He asked.

'I certainly hope so.'

Don't you just love it when things work out?

LAST MINUTE PREPARATIONS

'Damn these holiday makers!' Dorothy immediately felt ashamed of herself. She'd been one in Stackton herself in the days before the move, so knew only too well how important it could be to have that time away from everyday living. Was it always this busy, though? Surely, with this volume of humanity all milling around in the same spot, it couldn't be much respite from the humdrum task of conducting the regular tasks of one's daily living. 'When did normality become so difficult to handle?' she asked herself. Maybe it always was and it's only our perception that changes.

Having successfully negotiated her way through the crowds, she was relieved to take refuge in the travel agent's. Yes, of course she knew she could have booked her ticket online but didn't want to take any chances. Say she made a mistake and ended up in the wrong country? Say things went wrong with the baggage; and the check-in process these days! – well, last time she'd gone abroad, she'd arrived twenty five minutes before take-off, checked in and been on board quite comfortably. Now it took two hours just to get through the security checks – longer, much longer if the recent news reports were to be believed – and you had to arrive with your boarding card and everything already in your handbag. Dorothy was not an incompetent woman by any means, neither was she lazy or sloppy but this was just too important to leave to chance.

'A cocoa bean plantation. Really, how nice.' The agent didn't really have much interest in Dorothy's plans but did her best to appear fascinated without finding it easy to accomplish. She preferred booking people to go on beach holidays or places where there was a bit of sight-seeing. For her, travel should be about relaxation and whilst this client said it had been a lifetime passion, it was beyond her wit to imagine finding it remotely appealing watching a cocoa bean grow. Still, each to her own and if that's what the client wanted, that's what the client must have.

***

Amir was right and Ren vindicated in her attitude. 'Not eccentrics at all. Totally bloody barking bonkers.' Mrs Khan had been sorting out her washing. 'How do I manage to create so much of the wretched stuff?' she questioned. In order to make it a little less dull, she'd been listening to Classic FM, where it had just been announced that Ralph Vaughn Williams always wore odd socks. 'Maybe it made him first class composer,' she thought. On the other hand, maybe it made things worse, 'what with him having to spend all his time searching around for second identical pair'. But she suspected, staring down at the laundry basket, that was more likely to be Mrs V W's lot in life than his own.

Mrs Khan really didn't mind at all. She'd probably got any number of quirks only explicable to the rest of world as harmless oddities. 'Loveable barking bonkers, so all good.' She thought.

***

Looking more like the Cheshire cat than her usual somewhat dour self when she walked out of the agent's,

Dorothy made her way down to the seafront café and treated herself to a cappuccino – the real thing, not one of these skinny concoctions with no caffeine– and asked for LOADS of sprinkles and a lump of carrot cake. Everything was settled, even her currency had been arranged. Now it was so close, she was apprehensive but oh, so excited! It hadn't been at all easy finding a placement but wow! Guyana! For a whole month! What sights would she see and experiences would she have during that time? She was openly smiling at the visions passing in front of her mind's eye. She knew no-one who'd ever visited Guyana and loved the idea that she was going to achieve two 'firsts' in one go. Dorothy was not normally known as an innovator.

Sipping her coffee and watching the waves, she couldn't help looking back over the time since Mrs K – whom she now considered to be her 'dear friend' – had called her up and asked her what she thought about visiting a plantation. Never believing it would actually happen, she'd watched the other ladies all arriving at their goals and little by little had found her own resolve.

'Oh dear,' she thought, 'Bryony wouldn't like that. Not being called a lady.' But then, as Bryony wasn't there to read her mind, she turned back to watch the waves, contentedly luxuriating in her daydreams.

***

Lally and Chelsea were relieved that April Cottage was going to be their home for the foreseeable future. She and Del had put the old house on the market and Gos was moving out into the flat he'd found to rent in Bristol to be near his new job. He wouldn't be settling in permanently until the end of the summer, so they intended to continue seeing one another from time to time before the move.

'Will we still see uncle Gos when he doesn't live here anymore?' Chelsea wanted to know.

'I expect so, pet,' replied Lally, meaning 'I hope so.' 'He'll be coming to see Granny K, so we're bound to bump into him from time to time.' Please let it be more than that, she wished, not daring to pray in case whoever was up there took umbrage at being called upon only at those moments when she wanted something.

She was secretly hoping that Val would sell her April Cottage but wasn't ready to ask yet. Time enough for that once she'd settled Chelsea into her new school. Looking at her now, so grown up in her simple uniform of blue skirt and white blouse, bought this morning at the supermarket, 'Where did the time go?' she wondered. Oh Lally, we'd all like to know the same thing.

***

She and Mrs Khan had come to a firm decision to try to make a go of the tea blending. Valerie's shed was big enough for them to store most of the things they needed and between them, they could work something out. She'd never imagined she'd end up being a 'manufacturer' of anything, her primary ambition having been to have her own mobile hairdressing salon. It had all worked out perfectly, though, for she loved the contact with her clients, could organise her own working hours and it would keep her going while the tea business took off, if, indeed, it did. Being able to sell tea at W.I. fairs wasn't at all the same as being able to make it in the open market.

She and Helena had become firm friends while the two of them were studying in the same place. She hoped fervently that Helena would have the same sort of success as she was having herself. But Helena was one of those people that simply made things work and Lally was sure that her pursuit of fame would be no different.

**

After a wonderful day wandering around Steart Marshes, Val and Lawrence settled down for a quiet evening's relaxation. He switched on the radio and sat quietly listening to a programme about cork farming in the Algarve, Val quietly slumbering while lying across the sofa with her head in his lap.

I'd like to tell you that after a reasonable length of time, he swept her up in his arms, carefully carried her upstairs, gently laid her on the bed and sprinkled rose petals over the cover with angels singing, well, like angels, for the duration.

But what really happened was quite suddenly there was an almighty roar:

'Aarrgh! Oh hell! Get off my legs, Val! I've got cramp! Shift!' Valerie was awakened with a bump and unceremoniously thrown off her comfortable human cushion. When she sat up, Lawrence was jumping and bouncing around like one of those Mexican beans, screaming and hollering.

'Give me your foot. I'll stretch the muscle out for you,' she offered.

'Get off! Don't come near me!' This went on for some time but eventually he calmed down, visibly a little worse for wear.

The last thing Val heard in bed that night was 'First thing tomorrow, I'm going online to find out how to avoid cramp.'

Ah well, it can't all be sweet wine and red, red roses, can it.

THE FIRST STACKTON-ON-SEA
W.I. BUCKET LIST

Dear Members, Friends and Visitors

Over the last eighteen months, the members of Stackton-on-Sea W.I. have been working through their own Bucket List, inspired by our own Mrs Khan's mastery of the harp. There were no rules involved – the wish could be something tiny or mega-sized. The members have done their best to support and encourage each other with their endeavours and to date, the wishes have all been achieved.

GINA	Join Can't Sing Choir	YES
MAUREEN	Stratford theatre visit	YES
Dr DI	Narrowboat trip	YES
DI (the constable's wife)	Sports Day	YES
BETH	Nessie hunting	YES
LALLY	Complete hairdressing course	YES
DOROTHY	Cocoa bean plantation	August
KATHY	Start learning Spanish	YES
MOIRA	Have hair coloured with stripes	YES
JENNY	Walk a donkey	YES
STACKTON WI	Raise £10,000 for *the Let's Share Allotment*	YES!

We will be starting a new Bucket List for the coming year.
PLEASE COME ALONG AND MAKE YOUR OWN ENTRY
ON THE BUCKET LIST,
TAKE PART IN SOMEONE'S ELSE'S – OR EVEN BOTH?

HAPPY SUMMER!

Val Ford, outgoing President.

THE SUMMER FAIR

Picture this: a marquee bursting with stalls weighted down with every possible gift and luxury food item you can imagine. Lining the perimeter were stalls manned (Val felt sure that Bryony would insist on 'womanned') by W.I. members, each sporting summery clothes in primary colours alternating with shops from the town; in the centre, a refreshment stall serving drinks, cakes (obviously: how would they get through the day without them?) and, of course, the Stackton-on-Sea W.I. Special Blend Tea. Lally and Mrs Khan hadn't exactly worked hard on this particular creation but they'd done all they could to make the best possible tipple with the resources at their command, details of the recipe top secret, of course.

This was Val's last Summer Fair and it looked as if it would very likely be the best. She was relieved that it was the last real fixture of the season and glad that she'd be going out on a high note.

The only regular who was missing was Dr Di – having a wonderful time on a canal boat, so Val hoped – and each was supporting the event in their own particular fashion. Surely nothing could go wrong. What's that saying? The best laid plans of mice and man can go wrong. Well, let's see...

***

Wandering along the seafront, the Wizard wasn't finding it that easy to recover from his encounter with Helena, whom he'd decided was definitely a little unbalanced. What was making things worse was that his favourite bakery had run out of his all-time-favourite treat – thick, sticky mince slice, vegan, gooey and enormous, one cake would last four sittings. Well, two, anyway. Actually no. The intention was that it would provide him with more than one tooth-rotting snack (he described it thus in the vain hope it would discourage him from indulging too often) but the reality was that once he took that first bite, he couldn't possibly resist gobbling down the whole thing in one go and then going back to buy another one. He'd had to make do with a custard doughnut today. Really not the thing at all but beggars can't be choosers. He got a great dollop of custard in his beard, which did surprisingly little to enhance his appearance, the more so because he didn't realise it was there until it had gone solid and getting it out had meant cutting it out completely with a segment of facial hair. He'd heard that those two harpists were going to be in the W.I. tent, so he'd go and see if he could interest them in his venture to put Stackton-on-Sea on the map. Better approach the guy though. He'd had enough of having his ear chewed off by mad women. Surely someone in this town would appreciate what he was trying to do for it?

***

Chelsea had done enough behaving for one day. Lally and Mrs Khan were busy with the tea and all the other women were engaged on their various projects. Lally had hoped that when Bryony joined, it would be another woman to befriend, particularly as she had small children herself, so they could help each other out but Bryony had turned out to be something of an activist. Not that Lally was against making life better for women, far from it, but she didn't want to get involved in all that angry stuff that involved walking down the High Road with placards, chanting; and since Chelsea'd been born, she definitely didn't feel inclined to go bra-free.

As the women had arranged for a party for the garden gnomes (participation possible on donation by the owner to the charity fund), Gerald had been invited to attend. After all, he knew the predilections and foibles of the species better than any of them. He loved giving talks to W.I. meetings. They really got into the spirit of things and there were times when he wished he were brave enough to join, but in spite of his usual confidence, he didn't think he had it in him to be pioneer. His Day Job, from which he was now retired, had been as Head of a centre for youth rehabilitation. He'd been totally fulfilled and wouldn't have changed it for the world but now he felt the need to be a bit more light-hearted. These W.I. women certainly gave him every opportunity for that.

This afternoon, he'd been honoured to be asked to keep an eye on little Chelsea in the Gnome Enclosure. Of course, he wasn't on his own, Moira was there too, the same woman who'd asked about the pixies and goblins when he gave the talk. His own daughters were well and truly grown up and living in Scotland, so there was very little contact with the grandchildren, something he missed but knew that the girls had to make their own lives and for both it had meant a move to the other end of the country doing surveys, one on marine mammals, the other on insects. Gerald couldn't really see the attraction but who was he to interfere? At least the girls got on.

Gerald and Moira hit it off from the first moment and were enjoying swopping life stories with each other. Chelsea was having the best of times with the gnomes, chatting to them and feeding them imaginary ice creams and cakes. They could both see her out of the corners of their eyes but didn't want to get in the way of her games. Also, it gave them the chance to get to know each other a bit better. Whilst Moira was, by her own estimation, a happily married woman, it never did any harm to have extra friends, and her husband and Gerald might even get on. She hoped so. He didn't have many friends of his own and it would be good for both of them to have someone new in their social circle.

***

Mrs Khan and Lally were answering questions about the tea. Neither had envisaged this level of success. Lally's head was reeling with the possibilities. Her mother hadn't forgiven her for sending Del packing but what the hell? She'd never asked her for a single thing and had most certainly never been offered anything. She'd stopped even thinking about how she might be able to improve their relationship. Whilst willing to meet her halfway, she wasn't prepared to be the only one yielding ground and Mrs Varley was not going to be enticed into giving in to what she considered her daughter's whims.

Lally's happy demeanour was shattered when from nowhere she heard

'Lally! Come here. Come and see to Chelsea!' Fearing the worst, she tore out of the tea tent and sprinted over to the Gnomes' Tea Party narrowly avoiding knocking over half the assembled visitors.

There, she found that Chelsea had paired up all the gnomey revellers and had arranged them in varying attitudes worthy of a Gnome Kama Sutra.

***

'What is all fuss about?' asked Mrs Khan. 'We all got here by same means and produced others in like fashion.'

'Yes, Mrs Khan,' said Moira, 'but Chelsea's four years old and only starting school in a couple of months. This is *devious*.' She shuddered to think how she would have felt if her own kids had behaved in a like manner.

'Devious? Honestly? She has to learn sometime and this could save her from adding to the number of girls who fall pregnant by mistake and wished they hadn't.' Secretly, Mrs Khan was of the opinion that at four years old, conjugation with the opposite sex wasn't even the last thing on Chelsea's mind. Given that at her tender age she was barely articulate, Mrs K seriously doubted that her motivation had been anything more 'devious' than relieving her boredom and making a pretty tableau. She did believe, however, that knowing too much too soon was better than knowing too little too late.

'Mrs Healey,' said Mrs Khan, 'little Chelsea is budding biologist. She loves the birds and the bees. How could she possibly *not* be interested in how a species reproduces itself, even if species in question is *Gnomus gardenae*?'

'Mrs Khan. She's depicted them having s e x! This has nothing to do with reproducing the species!' Really? thought Mrs Khan, but simply said ' Would you prefer she had grouped them together to smoke or get drunk?'

'No, of course not but' – Mrs Khan wouldn't let her finish. 'Well then, best option chosen. No harm done.'

The gnomes were disengaged and their rightful owners – mostly chuckling to themselves – returned them safely to their usual habitats among the trees and flowers.

Thanks to Helena, the headline in the following Tuesday's paper read:

STACKTON-on-SEA W.I. HOSTS GNOME ORGY AT SUMMER FAIR.

Half of Stackton regretted they hadn't bother to go.

AUGUST

HAPPY DAYS!

Mrs Khan settled herself down under the parasol with a big jug of her special non-alcoholic fruit punch (recipe top secret but with copious dashes of squash and a sumptuous fruit salad floating on the top, all cooled by ice cubes as big as bricks) and pondered on the beauty of the garden at this special time of the year. The fuchsias were buzzing with bees and every flower bed and shrub was covered in colourful, sweet smelling blossom, all providing food for the insects and joy to the heart. She knew it was a cliché but her little patch of nature truly was an assault on the senses. 'Life is good,' she said, toasting all creation in her specially formulated elixir. 'And this drink isn't too bad, either,' she thought, pouring herself a second glass.

***

Valerie was feeling a little sad. Now that the end of her final year as President was effectively here, she was sorry to see it go. Still, she was intending to remain an active member, no matter how busy her life elsewhere. The new programme had been set and very interesting it looked.

Lawrence was going on three overseas tours with Brasso over the coming months, two of them quite long – three weeks each – and one of them four days. He'd suggested she go with him and she'd jumped at the chance, for the first one at least; and the short one, she hoped. She liked the company of his colleagues and was enjoying the open welcome they were extending to her. As well as that, the Choir were going to Sweden in November and she and Gina had been selected to go with them, no need to be reserves anymore. They'd found their feet as choristers and now they'd had their first taste of touring overseas on their visit to Spain, they'd overcome any fears of inadequacy and were confident and looking forward to being part of everything that the choir had to offer. On this occasion, the orchestra would be Swedish, so yet another new experience for them both was on the horizon. Mind you, saying it like that even to themselves, it sounded as if they were old hands, whereas they'd only sung in a small number of concerts to date, a dozen at the most. The choir had been booked for a show in the Cathedral in the run up to Christmas and had been invited to Wells to perform with yet another orchestra, so they were giving themselves over to it wholeheartedly and making the most of absolutely every single minute. As Gina's Bucket List entry had been to sing with a Can't Sing Choir, she was finding it a bit difficult to believe she hadn't fallen asleep and slipped down a rabbit hole. But no, she was definitely above ground.

Jenny was going to be an excellent President, of that Val was sure. All in all, the changes over the last year had been massive and positive and the catalyst for it all had been the indomitable Mrs Khan.

***

Gloria was anything but sad. She'd been invited by Jamie and Golnessa to spend the whole month with the two of them and four month old Freddie. 'We'd love to share this time with you, mum, and it would be great to have your experience to call on,' Jamie had told her. Goli had been calling out in the background that they wouldn't take no for an answer. 'Of course I'll come,' she answered, 'but if you get fed up with me, tell me so.' She hoped they wouldn't but watching the other women over the past year had taught her a lot. And of course, now she had an interest of her own, her everyday routine had changed all recognition. There was so much to it – it wasn't just creating an attractive design. There were all the calculations in respect of dimensions, for a start, and the 'brand image'. That had been really good fun to update, Dorothy having been using the same things ever since she retired. They wanted to keep it small and exclusive, like Ceyda's perfume business, only theirs wasn't a business of course but a cottage industry giving both of them pleasure and satisfaction. They worked well together and, she'd decided, Dorothy wasn't so bad really. It just took a bit of time to get to know her ways.

Gloria didn't bother to wonder about the future anymore, whether or not this newfound cordiality between her, Jamie and Golnessa would last but she'd do what she heard the others talking about and live for the minute. 'Do that,' Mrs K had told her, 'and the rest takes care of itself.'

All's well that ends well? Let's hope so.

***

Lawrence had decided that this was not the moment to be the New Version of Himself. 'My good man,' he said, adopting what he felt was an authoritative tone of voice and suitably condescending facial expression, 'since starting my professional career at the age of nineteen, I've played in the finest orchestras throughout the entire world under some of the greatest conductors who ever lived. I've played in all continents except for Antarctica both as a member of the band and a soloist. I've been named on over three hundred recordings – *maybe a little bit of an exaggeration, he thought* – and have offers of work for the next four years. Thank you for your interest but no.' With that, he got up and left his coffee untouched.

THE END OF THE BEGINNING

As Dorothy stepped out of the taxi to pick up her flight for Georgetown, she couldn't help thinking it was a mistake not to have taken up the offers by members of the WI, several of whom had suggested they accompany her to the airport. They'd wanted to see her off and wish her bon voyage. She was still apprehensive, still excited and still couldn't believe it was really her setting out on this incredible journey. It was a long time since she'd even had a proper holiday and this one was, well, to describe it as the holiday of a lifetime was the very soul of inadequacy.

She checked in and went over to buy herself a hot chocolate – what else? – from one of the more pleasant-seeming cafes. There's not really any need to tell you that it didn't begin to compare with the ones she magicked up herself, but it did the trick. She felt sure she'd seen that dreadful man with the beard that provided a resting place for all manner of biscuits and every possible variation of cooked egg. He was talking animatedly to the poor girl at the desk, seemingly arguing about the fifteen or so trunk-sized suitcases he had with him. 'Well, let's hope he's found someone else to persecute,' she thought, 'we don't need him here.'

Sitting on the plane, mulling over what might be in the presentation she was going to make at the October meeting, she decided that although it sounded a bit diva-ish and melodramatic, the past year had literally changed her and made her life into something hitherto the stuff of dreams she'd never even dared to dream. She could never have conjured up the idea of any of this and yet now, here it was, unfolding like a lotus flower. Who'd have thought such a quiet, unassuming woman as Mrs K would have influenced all their lives so much and so positively, and without any fanfare or displays of ostentation.

Their futures looked bright indeed.

***

In the spare bedroom of her tiny flat, Helena had her email account open. The one she was staring at in her inbox was practically burning her eyes. She knew she'd have to open it soon or consign it to the junk file without discovering its contents. 'Here goes,' she told the ether.

'Hi Helena,
We'd like to invite you back for further tests. Please call us on the number below'

She knew she'd never get it but still, this was much more than she'd allowed herself to hope for. Fillers, indeed. The man was clearly living in a world of make-believe. She felt vindicated.

***

Mrs Khan and Lally were playing with Chelsea, watching her run around the garden talking to the plants and helping her make bouquets to take home for her dolls. Lally was almost at optimum capacity with hairdressing clients and jogging along nicely. Once the new term started, Chelsea would be off to school five mornings a week and continuing to accompany her mother on afternoon hair-dressing visits until she went full time later in the year. 'A daughter at school five whole days a week,' thought Lally with a wistful smile. 'It's quite true what they say. They're grown up before you know it.' Lally and Del had agreed that he should have as much access in terms of visiting and days out as he wanted but it would be too disruptive for Chelsea to be swopped between two households, so it had all worked out amicably in the end. Even her mother couldn't complain but it hadn't stopped her trying.

'It's been a lovely year, Mrs Khan.' Said Lally. 'It could have been a disaster but instead, it's been a proper new start.'

Mrs Khan poured the three of them another glass of fruit punch and they spent a pleasant couple of hours chatting and enjoying the summer sun. As she watched Lally and Chelsea, she, too, couldn't help wondering what the future would hold, now that Ren was definitely staying in America with her new man. The grandchildren were adults, so they were starting out on lives of their own, eager to prove themselves in an increasingly complex and challenging world. Disappointing in one way but in another, she had high hopes. As it wasn't her place to interfere, she'd never said a word.

The next day, Mrs Khan had an early start. Gos got her to the airport exactly on time, removed his mother's cases from the boot of the car and wheeled them over to the luggage check-in. He plonked one last kiss on her cheek and giving her a cheery wave called out 'Have a wonderful time, mum! See you in a month!'

Gita was going to meet her at the Airport. They were going back to the old family home, where Mrs Khan had grown up and Gita had lived her whole life. Never having married, she'd taken over the management of the plantation and was making a real success of it. Romesh had never been interested in tea, so in spite of it being the usual thing for the eldest son – only, in this case – to take things over, he'd happily signed it over to Gita, on the understanding that he could still have a small villa for whenever he visited. He was in Australia working in IT and rarely made it back.

Mrs Khan settled into her seat and determined that she'd sleep all the way. She wanted to be bright and fresh when she arrived.

'I am so privileged to be living my life,' she thought as she started to give in to drowsiness, 'and so lucky to have found Stackton-on-Sea W.I. with all its fun and intrigue.' With that happy thought nestling down in the recesses of her brain, she drifted off into a contented, dream-filled slumber and didn't wake again until the plane touched down on the tarmac.

STACKTON-ON-SEA WI
Programme 2022-2023

All meetings 2-4pm (unless stated otherwise) in the W.I. Hut

September 8th	PROBLEMS IN THE PIT Disasters in the orchestra pit at an Opera House and how to resolve them
September 24th 10am-4pm	PERFUME MAKING WORKSHOP PLEASE BRING YOUR OWN LUNCH Donations towards materials and use of hut
October 11th	GLORIOUS GUYANA A special talk by Dorothy about her visit to a cocoa bean plantation
October 22nd 10am-4pm	CHRISTMAS CRAFTS WORKSHOP, INCLUDING CARDS AND UNUSUAL EVERGREEN WREATHS PLEASE BRING YOUR OWN LUNCH Donations towards materials and use of hut welcome
November 8th	STUFFING WORKSHOP
November 11th	SPECIAL BUCKET LIST EVENING Our members will be talking about their experiences. Come along and see what they've achieved. SNACKS PROVIDED —please let us know if you can help with the catering
November 27th 10am-4pm	CHRISTMAS FAIR
December 6th 1pm.	CHRISTMAS LUNCH

January 10th	<u>PAMPER AFTERNOON</u> Hand/head massage, manicure, pedicure PLEASE BOOK – donations for materials would be welcome
February 7th	<u>THE BRIDGWATER CARNIVAL</u> – could we do it here in Stackton?
March 7th	<u>CHEESE MAKING IN CHEDDAR</u>
April 11th	<u>IS THERE ANYBODY OUT THERE?</u> The case for extra-terrestrial life
May 9th	<u>MY LIFE IN TV</u> Helena will be telling us what it's like being a presenter on Golden Days TV
May 13th 10am-4pm	<u>CRAFT DAY FOR THE SUMMER FAIR</u> Please let the Committee know what you would like to make
June 13th	<u>THE WILDLIFE OF THE CANAL</u>
July 1st 10am-2pm	<u>SUMMER FAIR IN THE MARQUEE</u> All other fixtures will be announced in monthly meetings and circulated via email. Please ensure we have your up-to-date email address.

PLEASE NOTE: *THE COMING YEAR LOOKS AS IF IT WILL BE EVEN BUSIER THAN LAST YEAR, NOW THAT WE ARE EMBARKING ON THE SECOND INCARNATION OF THE W.I. BUCKET LIST. ANYONE INTERESTED IN EITHER ADDING TO THE LIST OR TAKING PART IN ANY OF THE ACTIVITIES OFFERED BY ANOTHER MEMBER, PLEASE LET THE COMMITTEE KNOW IN THE USUAL WAY.*

WE ARE STILL LOOKING FOR ANOTHER RESERVE FOR THE EGGHEADS TEAM. PLEASE GIVE HELENA YOUR NAME AS SOON AS POSSIBLE, SO SHE CAN GO AHEAD AND APPLY.

EPILOGUE

The editor of the Stackton-on-Sea Chronicle looked aghast.

'There's been loads of interest in these women.' She told him. 'Not just us, but on TV; and you hear people talking about them all the time.' She hadn't expected to have an easy time convincing him, so she was well prepared.

'So let's just get this straight. You want me to give you time off so you can write a book about these girls.' The poor man had to sit down in case the shock of the insanity of it all caused him to keel over and die. 'You want to "tell their story". Do you seriously think anyone would want to read it?'

'Of course they would. It's a serious celebration of reaching mature years and of the benefits of the mixing of generations.'

Dick Dastardly (as he was affectionately known) could think of nothing about reaching 'mature years' that was worth celebrating. But then, he was barely out of his twenties.

'Maybe I could be freelance for a month or something. Go part-time, anything.'

'How long do you envisage it taking?' asked Dick.

'Not long.' How long is a piece of string? She thought, making a mental note to steer clear of clichés once she started writing. 'We could make it one of the SC's publications, generate some income for the paper.' He was always saying how difficult it was keeping the Chronicle going, what with everyone competing to get at the same limited pool of advertising and the internet and television being so much more immediate.

'Oh all right, if you must. I'm a fool to myself. Give me a couple of days and come back to me on it. I'll see if I can sort something out.'

She took this as a sign it was definitely going to happen with Dick's blessing. 'It'll be a great project,' she said curbing the instinct to bop round the room singing. 'You'll see! I won't let you down!' She set to getting all her source materials together and working out how she was going to do it. Convincing him had been easier than she'd bargained for and she was keen to make a good job of it, not least of all so that she could justify his faith in her.

'Just think of what fortune it could bring for the Stackton Chronicle if the film rights are sold', she thought. 'I wonder if Meera Syal might be tempted to age and play Mrs Khan?'

ACKNOWLEDGEMENTS

Rebecca Brown - for getting the book into publishable form and doing such a great job.

Cheryl May – for inviting me to the Monday writing group, where we have a lot of fun. Also to Alan, Ann, Chris, Davina, Jean. John, Pam, Peter, Ros, both for being part of the group and being great people to hang out with.

Jean Owen – for reading the novel for me with an editor's eye, feeding back and giving advice.

Scott at Ravenprint, for all the seemingly endless tweaks and refinements!

Ros Whistance – for helping and encouraging, and to Dave, her husband, who has the patience of a saint.

Paula Yard – for helping me to sort out cocoa bean plantations in Guyana! This wasn't an easy task, as there are very few and the most recent internet references relate to 2017.

All my friends, far too numerous to mention here, for help, encouragement, and simply making the going easier when it was necessary to have a boost.

-----coming soon

VOICES

Polly J. Fry was a singer.
Acting on an extremely foolish whim, she damaged her voice
and was unable to sing for sixteen years.
Voices is a three part narrative exploring the
process of learning to accept that her voice was gone, the
even greater trauma of rebuilding it once it had resur-
faced and the years between.

Interspersed among Fry's own story are bite-sized fic-
tional tales, microworlds vividly
painted - her signature format. The exploits of the
delightful, if rather extraordinary, Grannie Louie con-
trast with stories of romance, comedy, drama; and the
everyday experiences of ordinary people.

A worthy sequel to Fry's *Wyddershyns*.

Printed in Great Britain
by Amazon